DEMON MOON

XOE MEYERS - BOOK ONE

SARA C. ROETHLE

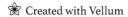 Created with Vellum

1

I stared up at the moon, partially obscured by ominous looking clouds. I brushed a loose flake of ash from my hair as I tried to forget the overwhelming, acrid stench of smoke that had nearly overcome my lungs. I shivered. At least I was still alive. I blearily thought back over the past week, knowing my life would never be the same again.

ANOTHER YEAR at Shelby Heights High School in not-so-sunny Shelby, Oregon . . . oh joy. Shelby isn't exactly a small town, but it's definitely not a city. I'm not much of a "people-person", so the size is one of the few things I like about Shelby. That, and the woods that surround it. Tall pine trees are never out of reach. I've always been outdoorsy. My dad took off shortly after I was conceived and my mom raised me on camping trips and hiking. My name's Alexondra Meyers, by the way. I know, it's pretty horrible. Mercifully, the few friends I have call me Xoe.

Back to the matter at hand . . . junior year. I am not a fan of high school, or the teenage experience in general. I don't consider myself antisocial, though most of my fellow students might argue that point. Really, I just don't like to waste my time with pretense. Why bother being nice to someone I secretly dislike? Why engage in small talk if nothing meaningful is accomplished? I'd rather have a few real friends than a bunch of fake ones.

I trudged toward the towering, gray brick monstrosity that was Shelby High, feeling morose. Where there wasn't sidewalk or asphalt, the ground was covered with lush, green grass. Shelby is always green and moist, which is nice, except for the mold and mildew that tend to grow if you're not careful. Once my mom got a new car windshield that wasn't sealed properly. Within weeks the insides of her windows had grown algae.

I forced my sneakered feet to continue forward, concentrating on the sound of my footfalls, one foot in front of the other. As I approached the dreaded double-doors, my best friend Lucy joined me. We usually walked to school together, but Lucy always arrived at school early on the first day. She liked to "prepare" her locker and map out all of her classes beforehand. She's a bit of an over achiever, to put it mildly.

Lucy and I pushed through the double doors together. I held onto my door long enough for a girl with a mass of brown curls to grab it and keep it open for herself. See? Not antisocial. I glanced down at the top of Lucy's dark-haired head as we made our way down the hall.

Lucy and I are complete opposites when it comes to appearance. I'm a giant compared to her. Well, not really a giant, but her petite 5'1" frame makes my willowy 5'8" seem excessive. Her long, dark, glossy hair is in complete contrast to my shaggy, shoulder-length, white-blonde mop. Lucy's skin is deep olive all year round, whereas mine is pale, and at times, a little pasty, what my mom kindly refers to as *porcelain.* Did I say that I'm a little jealous of Lucy? If I didn't love her so much, I would probably hate her.

Lucy had chosen dark wash jeans with a pale blue button-up blouse for her first day attire. The tips of conservative brown shoes peeked out from the bottom of her jeans. Lucy's sense of style errs on the side of caution. Her pin-straight hair was parted down the middle to cascade nearly to her waist, framing her fine-boned, delicate face, void of make-up.

Lucy's almond-shaped brown eyes peered up into my large green ones, waiting for my whining to begin. She'd had to deal with my complaining on the first day of school every year since second grade. We'd become friends when my mom and I first moved to Shelby, as Lucy's family lives just down the street from us. Alone and friendless, I had gone exploring in the woods behind my house, against my mom's strict commands, and Lucy was doing the same. We both had a stubborn independent streak that constantly ordered us to disobey our parents. How could we not be friends?

I glanced out the windows at the other end of the hall as we moved to stand in front of Lucy's locker. To add to my first day misery, the sky above Shelby was an angry gray, promising rain. Black clouds rolled ominously in the distance. So what else was new? I hate the rain. I'm not like a girly-girl that's afraid to get my hair wet or anything, but I'm at my happiest when I'm outdoors, and it's not terribly pleasant to be outside when it's raining. So, despite my pallid appearance, I much prefer the sun. I took a deep breath of the ozone-scented air that flowed in every time the doors opened. Let the whining commence.

"It's not that bad," Lucy consoled, taking in my grimace. "We have three classes together and you have two more with Allison. That leaves only one class to trudge through without us."

Allison was another on my short list of friends, though I'd only known her since freshman year. Lucy and I had met her during our first lunch at Shelby High. Allison's family was new to Shelby, so she didn't know anyone. Rather than taking a seat at one of the loner tables, she had marched right up to where Lucy and I sat, slammed her tray down, and began chatting away like she had known us for years. I was skeptical of Allison's blunt style of friendship at first, but she turned out to be genuine. Plus, she adds a little bit of girliness to our small group.

"A small consolation at best," I replied sullenly as I looked up at the numbers on the wall of lockers, wondering where mine would be that year.

Lucy hummed happily as she opened her locker and pulled out the book needed for her first class. Her eternally sunny attitude could be quite vexing at times. Though, if she were a pessimist like me, the complaining would never cease. Lucy's glass half full philosophy made my glass look empty, dirty, and cracked.

Turning to me to take in my dejected expression, Lucy frowned. "I'll see you in French."

I managed a small smile, despite my misery. "See you then."

We parted ways as the first bell rang, and ran toward our respective classes to the sound of clanging lockers and hurried *see you laters*. I still hadn't found my locker, but it would have to wait.

I trailed my fingertips across the aged walls as I walked, in no real hurry to get to class. Shelby High is old, and I mean *old.* I could feel the bumps of count-less layers of peeling paint beneath my fingers. The newest layer of paint was a pale yellow that was trying hard to be cheery, but fell a little short. I went past a row of faded green lockers, then took a left into my classroom.

My first class of the day, which I had with Allison, was biology. I scowled as I entered the classroom. It was simply too early in the morning for science. The room boasted lab tables instead of desks, making the space feel even more small and cramped than normal classrooms. The buzzing of the fluorescent lights mixed with the din of murmured voices made me feel instantly claustrophobic. I searched across the tables, which were set up to seat two people, with a little sink and electrical outlets in the middle, until my eyes landed on Allison. She waved me over to the table she had reserved for us at the back of the room.

I liked sitting in the back of the class. I don't enjoy the feeling of people's eyes on the back of my head, and teachers usually tend to call on people in the front of the class, ignoring the back. It's not that I don't understand the questions, I just prefer not to answer them. Allison was more than willing to sit in the back of the class with me.

Lucy was a whole other story. I always tried to lure her to the back, the *Dark Side* as far as she was concerned. We ended up front and center every time, where she could be sure the teacher called on her when she raised her hand to answer every question. But hey, she diverts the teacher's attention from me, so I can't really complain.

As I approached, Allison looked me up and down,

ending with a look of distaste at my ratty old sneakers. "Xoe, we are going shopping this weekend, no arguments."

Smirking, I looked down at my dark blue, vintage *Doors* tee and holey jeans, then at her blue sundress with strappy dark brown sandals, artfully applied makeup, and perfectly styled, long, honey blonde hair. Unlike me, Allison embraces the blonde. She is the master of the hair flip. I've never felt like a "blonde", but I'm too pale to pull off much of anything else, so I just try to ignore it.

At 5'6" Allison almost reaches my height, though she has a few more curves than I do, perfectly accentuated by her dress. She was still staring at my outfit with a perfectly arched eyebrow raised. Maybe Allison had a point. *Maybe.*

"Sure Allison, whatever you say." I was keeping the sneakers no matter what clothes she tried to put me in. They were my tried and true favorites, perfectly broken in and shaped to my feet. They had started life a solid black, but had faded to what I considered a rather pleasant gray. Allison took one last look at me, pity in her blue eyes, then turned toward the front of the class.

A throat cleared, bringing my attention to where our teacher, Mrs. Sanders, was waiting. Mrs. Sanders taught both biology and microbiology at Shelby Heights. She was a short, dare I say dumpy kind of woman with a horribly monotonous voice. She stared at me in mock exasperation until I slumped dejectedly into my hard plastic chair.

Mrs. Sanders went on to drone for an hour about her syllabus and all that other nonsense, with occasional pauses to straighten her lumpy pink cardigan. I drew on the cover of my notebook and tried to ignore her. By the time class was near its end, my notebook was covered with a mish-mash of nonsensical doodles.

Impatient for the bell to ring, I shoved my books back into the green backpack I used every year, throwing my pencil in haphazardly on top. I watched the clock, counting away the final seconds of class.

Finally the bell rang, and it was off to my next two hours of torture: French and World History. Even though I'd be with Lucy, I knew time would creep by at an alarmingly slow rate. I'm horrible at French, the pronunciation is simply beyond me, and World History is, well, World History. When I entered my French class, Lucy was already sitting front and center. Her new navy blue backpack was sitting in the seat next to her, waiting for me to take its place. After what seemed like days of words I didn't understand, followed by a lengthy discussion on "the cradle of civilization", it was finally time for lunch—my brief reprieve from the monotony.

The cafeteria is one of the few spacious areas in Shelby High. The brightly lit fluorescents are diffused by the copious amount of natural light that pours in from several large single-pane windows mounted in two of the walls. My little group always claimed the same table at the beginning of each year. It was in a corner, so we only had to deal with two other tables near us, rather than four. We were also stationed directly below one of the aforementioned windows. Said window looked out over the courtyard area of Shelby High, which is basically just a large square of grass with several picnic tables stationed in the center. On rare sunny days we would eat outside.

Occasionally other acquaintances would sit with us, but most of the time it was just us three, and that was the way we liked it. Well, *I* liked it at least. Allison and Lucy are slightly more social than I am.

Lucy and I waited at our usual table with our bagged lunches while Allison bought hers. Allison's willingness to eat school lunches made me seriously question her sanity. Let's just say they weren't always identifiable as food products. Her justification was that she didn't *do* lunchboxes.

Bored, I scanned the lunch line for Allison, but a boy staring in my direction caught my eye first. He stood watching me with an empty tray in his hands, reminding me of a robot or some other mindless automaton. His short, near-black hair was styled to perfection. His pale blue eyes, emphasized by a deep tan, stared intensely at me. His stood at around 6'3" with a hulking frame that strained against a plain gray tee-shirt, topped by a simple brown leather jacket.

As I observed him he continued to stare, pursing

his full lips that I imagined would be stuck in a perpetual pout. Besides the lips, the rest of his face was the epitome of masculinity: high, sculpted cheek bones, defined jaw-line, and a strong nose.

His heavy gaze sent a chill up my spine. What a creep. His husky-like eyes left me to land on Lucy, who he stared at just as intensely. I looked away with a scowl to finish scanning the lunch line for Allison. She had already paid and was walking toward our table.

"Oh come on," Allison said as she approached and noticed my scowl, "your day could not have been that bad."

Turning my scowl into a grin, I taunted, "Don't worry Al, it'll get better. We have gym next."

Allison's mocking smile faded. She whipped her hair over her shoulder and sat down next to me as she placed her lunch tray on the table. "Gee, Xoe, thanks for reminding me, and don't call me Al."

Gym was the bane of Allison's existence, as was my habit of calling her Al. She wasn't into sports of any kind, though she would probably be pretty good at them if she actually tried. Contrary to her tastes as a seemingly traditional girly girl, she was one of the toughest people I had ever met, and would probably kick butt at some of the more aggressive sports if she actually tried. She was definitely not a book to be judged by its cover.

Unlike Allison, I actually liked gym. With my height and a fair amount of coordination, I'm decent at sports, and gym doesn't require hours of boring teaching. I have trouble sitting still for too long.

Allison turned to Lucy. "So Xoe and I are going shopping this weekend. You in?"

Lucy turned a speculative eye to me. "Xoe? Shopping? My how the times have changed."

I pursed my lips into an exaggerated pout. "I need new socks."

Lucy laughed. "Ah, the truth comes out." Then turning back to Allison added, "I'll come. I need a new toothbrush."

Allison crossed her arms and glared back and forth between us. "You're both updating your wardrobes if it's the last thing I do. I feel less fashionable just sitting near you."

Lucy rolled her eyes at me as Allison changed the subject to how her day had been so far. As Allison prattled on, I looked over my shoulder to scan the cafeteria for the creepy staring guy. I spotted him almost immediately sitting with Max, a J.V. soccer player, and yep, still staring.

Noticing my distraction, Allison took a break from her monologue to turn and follow my gaze. "Who's the hunk?"

"That *creep* has been staring over here since we sat down," I grumbled.

Allison smirked. "He's hot, maybe you should go teach him some manners."

I raised an eyebrow at her comment. "I will never

understand your taste in men. He looks like an overly-primped jerk."

Allison raised both of her eyebrows in surprise. "My Xoe, you sure are feeling judgy today. That's supposed to be my job." She rose from her seat and looked over at Creepy Guy.

Realizing her intent, I reached for her arm and tried to pull her back down. "No way Al," I chided. "Don't even think about it."

Ignoring my comment, Allison pulled her arm away from me. With a mischievous smile, she hustled away from our table, then waltzed right up to Creepy Guy. She sat down on the other side of his table, facing him and Max companionably.

I shook my head and turned back to Lucy. We exchanged similar looks of resignation.

I sighed loudly. "And so it begins."

Lucy began to reply, then quickly turned her gaze down to the tabletop. I turned partially around to see what had interrupted Lucy. Allison was walking toward us, leading Creepy Guy by the hand. They came to stand at the head of our table.

Allison twined her arm through Creepy Guy's, which remained limp. "Girls, this is Dan. He's new here." Allison nodded in Lucy's direction. "That's Lucy," then nodded to me, "and that lovely example of radiant good cheer is Xoe."

Allison released Dan's arm and took a seat next to Lucy, leaving only one option for Dan. I had a moment to glare at Allison for her cruelty, then Dan sat next to me with a quizzical look, like he didn't quite know what I was. I quickly turned away and found my gaze wandering back to Max, who was now sitting alone, looking confused. He stood and walked straight out of the cafeteria like a sleepwalker. I stared for a moment at the now empty doorway, wondering what had gotten into Max to make him act so strangely.

When I turned back to our table, I noticed Dan's gaze had drifted to Lucy. The look he gave her was far different from the confused one he had given me. He looked at Lucy like she was a piece of meat, and he wasn't even trying to hide it.

I expected Lucy to be squirming under the pressure of Dan's gaze, but instead she offered him a coy smile. My mouth fell open in surprise. I'd never seen Lucy flirt before, and I couldn't believe she'd chosen that moment to start. Dan didn't really seem her type, though I didn't actually know what her type was. Lucy, like me, didn't date a lot.

Allison, on the other hand, I was used to. She flirted up dates on a regular basis, and had no problem talking to guys. She was born to flirt, and flirt she did.

Before I knew what had happened, Allison's flirting magic had involved Dan in our shopping plans for the weekend, which had been altered to movie plans . . . gre-at. I would have rather gone shopping, and that was saying a lot. Dan had not made a good first impression on me.

My own thoughts began to tune out the conversation as Allison continued to quiz Dan on where he was from and any other inane fact she could think of. I felt uncomfortable sitting next to Dan. Waves of creepiness emanated from him. Okay, so maybe "waves of creepiness" was a little dramatic, but there was something very strange about him. He made my skin crawl. He shifted so that his elbow brushed mine, and I struggled not to rub the goose bumps that instantly erupted on my arms.

I scooted away and watched him have a seemingly normal conversation with Lucy and Allison, while I tried to pinpoint what had me on edge. Listening to him talk, he seemed perfectly normal, but his face shattered the illusion. His gaze never left Lucy, even when he was answering one of Allison's questions. It was like he was trying to memorize every small detail of her face. It was downright unnerving.

The bell rang, startling me. I stood abruptly and gathered up my uneaten lunch, grateful for once that lunchtime was over. Ignoring Dan, I said bye to Lucy, then grabbed onto Allison, who was entering Dan's phone number into her cell. As soon as she finished, I hurried her away from our table, leaving Dan and Lucy behind. I could feel the electric pressure of Dan's eyes on us the entire way.

"Isn't he gorgeous?" Allison swooned once we were out in the hall and clear from Dan's gaze.

"What?" I questioned, lost in thought.

"Dan! He's gorgeous, or weren't you at the same lunch table as me?"

Allison liked Creepy Guy? Was she blind? The way he looked at Lucy had been pretty hard to miss. "Are you kidding? He's a total weirdo. Did you see the way he watched Lucy? Why did you have to invite him this weekend?"

"Oh Xoe," Allison responded, "ever the pessimist. Just give him a chance. It'll be fun." She paused for a moment and squinted her eyes. "And yes, I noticed the staring, but it doesn't mean he likes Lucy. It could mean anything."

"I didn't mean it that way," I clarified. "It was eerie. He hardly blinked. He looked at her like his favorite possession."

Allison frowned as a girl trying to get to her locker bumped into her. "Maybe he was just nervous."

"That was *so* not nerves," I argued. "That was stalker potential."

"You're being paranoid, Xoe. He just didn't know how to act. It's his first day at a new school. I'm sure he's fine," Allison paused. "You don't have to come on Saturday if you don't want to."

I set my jaw stubbornly. "No, I'll be there."

I was coming all right. I'd be damned if that creep was going to cause me to stay home on a Saturday, even if I had to sit through an entire chick-flick. Plus, how else was I supposed to keep an eye on him? Now, if only the feeling of doom in my gut would agree with me.

We made our way to the gymnasium, then headed straight to the girl's locker room to change. The gym somehow seemed even older than the rest of the school. You could feel the years of tears and sweat that had gone into the place, giving it an almost electric buzz. The walls had received the same lovely paint treatment as the rest of the building, and the gloss on the hardwood floors had been all but worn away by the thousands of feet that passed before us.

Our school was small enough that our gym classes were co-ed. It had been an issue with some of the parents,as apparently it was taboo for boys and girls to see each other in gym clothes, but common sense won out. I would never understand parents. The co-ed classes were fine by me. The more competition, the better.

I changed my clothes quickly, grateful that we were allowed to wear our own sweats. The uniforms the school supplied were reused each year and came in our school colors of yellow and green. Yuck. How yellow and green went with our school mascot, an eagle, was beyond me. I let my dingy gray tee shirt fall over my plain black sweats and tied my hair in as much of a ponytail as its length would allow. I turned to Allison as I sat to tie my *Nike* tennis shoes, to see her dressed in pink shorts and a fitted white t-shirt, with a look of grim determination on her face. To Allison, preparing for gym class was akin to preparing for battle. We walked back into the gym as Mr. "Call me Mitch" Walters was announcing that today was volleyball day. Most excellent.

Brian Fletcher was chosen as one of the team captains. Brian and I go way back. He's my next-door neighbor and has been since I moved to Shelby. I've been friends with him about as long as I have Lucy. Brian's smiling brown eyes landed on me as he chose me for his first teammate. I jogged up to stand beside him and ruffled his curly brown hair with my hand. Brian didn't only choose me because I'm his friend, I also kick butt at volleyball, and he's almost as competitive as I am. To say we like to win is a vast understatement.

Allison was usually chosen last for team sports. She tends to close her eyes and flinch any time a ball comes near her. When the choices were down to Allison and a small nerdy boy I didn't know, Brian finally put Allison on our team. She shuffled up to stand by me as Brian ran to the ball rack to grab a few volleyballs.

Play began and I was up to serve first. I hit the ball overhand, aiming right at the small nerdy boy. He ducked out of the way, not even trying to hit the ball. Point one for us. So maybe I played a little dirty. So what? My teammates never complained.

After we started to play, time went by in a flash, and we totally crushed the opposition. Soon we only had 10 minutes of class left, not enough to play another game, so "Mitch" told us just to get changed and hang out until the bell rang.

No one takes showers after gym class. It may seem kind of gross, but if you could see the rusty, grime-infested showers in the Shelby High locker rooms, you would no doubt understand. The consensus was that you would come out dirtier than when you went in.

Having changed back out of our gym clothes, Al and I went to stand near the door to talk to Brian. We had barely reached Brian when Cindy Miller swayed up to us. As gym was the bane of Allison's existence, so Cindy Miller was the bane of mine. Cindy was every guy's dream and my worst nightmare, rolled up into a slim brunette package.

Completely ignoring Al and me, Cindy walked up to Brian. "Nice game," she purred. "we should practice together sometime." As she spoke, Cindy casually brushed imaginary lint off Brian's shoulder.

Brian looked at me pleadingly, trapped. I tapped Cindy on the shoulder, turning her to me with a look of distaste in her large brown eyes.

"*What*?" She asked with as much snark as a single word could possibly possess, snarling her glossed lips.

"Oh, I thought you were asking Brian for some playing tips," I replied sweetly. "I was going to tell you to keep your head down. It's rather large and blocks your teammates' view of the ball, though the same tip could apply to your butt as well." I gave her my most innocent smile.

Catty, I know, but Cindy had it coming. Last year she spread a rumor that Allison was bulimic, and purposefully dumped a soda onto me during lunch. So *me-ow*. Cindy gave me a murderous look and walked away as Allison burst into laughter.

Brian put his arm around my shoulders companionably. "That's why we love you, Xoe."

The bell rang and Brian gave me a quick kiss on the cheek, then practically skipped away to his locker like an excited puppy. He had English with me next. Now don't get the wrong idea, Brian and I were strictly friends. We had more of a brother-sister relationship. People talk, as people tend to do, but we'd never crossed that friendship line. I said goodbye to Allison, then headed to class.

I reached my English class and snagged a seat near the back, though the very back row was already full, so I had to settle for the second to last row. I was patiently waiting for the "excitement" to begin when, lo and behold, Creepy Guy, I mean Dan, walked in. He walked right toward me, then took the open seat to my right. I froze, like a mouse trying not to draw the cat's attention. He glanced at me, as if to say something. With my heart pounding in my ears, I ignored him, keeping my eyes toward the front of the class.

Brian came rushing in and took the seat on my other side, oblivious to my predicament. As class began, I noticed Dan sneaking more puzzled glances at me. Squinting his pale blue eyes, he would tilt his head slightly, almost like a dog. My wardrobe might have been a little out of style, but was it really that puzzling? Did I have something on my face? The weird looks were starting to get to me.

Brian passed me a note while the teacher's back was turned. I opened it and read, "What's with that guy?"

I gave Brian an exasperated look and shrugged, relieved that it wasn't just in my head. I turned my eyes to the front of class and prepared to wait out the rest of the torturous hour.

When the bell finally rang, Dan reached out as if to grab my arm, with a calculating look in his eyes. I quickly turned away from him to Brian, and practically dragged Brian out of class. The look in Dan's eyes as he'd reached for me had been completely alien, like he had dropped his already poor mask of normalcy. Whatever lurked behind those icy blue eyes wasn't something I knew how to deal with.

Brian and I stopped in the hall, safely away from the classroom, to discuss the creepiness of Dan. With a nervous look over my shoulder, I dragged Brian a little farther away from the classroom, just as Dan exited and walked past us. "Allison invited him to the movies with us this weekend," I whispered, making it clear by my tone that the movie date was a bad thing.

Brian frowned. "That does *not* seem like a good idea. I've got a bad feeling about him."

At least someone agreed with me. "You know how Allison is . . . "

Brian smiled ruefully. "Yeah, I guess you didn't have much choice. I could come with you, just in case."

"Really?" Maybe things were looking up. "We're going Saturday evening."

He cringed. "Oh. Sorry Xoe . . . football practice." He shrugged and bit his lip. "I could cancel . . . "

"No, no it's okay," I assured. "I'm sure we're just being paranoid."

Brian nodded slowly, still hesitating. He nodded again and stood up a little straighter, as if making up his mind. "C'mon, I'll walk you to class."

Brian and I walked in silence the short distance to my geometry class. He stopped me before I walked into the classroom. "If you change your mind and want me to come, just call."

I had begun to say thanks just as Allison whipped by us, grabbing my arm and dragging me into the classroom. I waved to Brian as he turned to go to his next class.

Allison and I snagged seats in the back just as the bell rang. She turned to me and opened her mouth as if to speak, but the teacher began her lecture, sealing any chance Allison had to talk. Assuming she was probably going to talk about Dan, I didn't really mind. Allison crossed her arms and slouched down in her chair, seeming more than a little sullen. I looked out the window to our green surroundings and daydreamed for the rest of class, glad that I was no longer in the same room as Dan.

After geometry, Allison had to rush to her year-book committee meeting and I went to find Lucy. Lucy was already waiting outside the school entrance when I arrived, just like she always was. We started the short walk to our houses in silence, passing through the parking lot in front of the school, then veering away from the road to cut through the woods. We could get home following the road, but taking the trail through the woods cut about ten minutes off our journey.

Before Allison got her car, she would insist on the longer route of paved road whenever she came home with us, as Allison isn't big on the woods. They get her shoes dirty.

Lucy and I walked along companionably, shaded by the pine trees that bordered either side of the partially grown-over trail. A narrow strip of deep brown soil was all that was left to show us the way, though we'd walked it so many times we didn't need the trail to lead us home. I looked up through the trees to find that the sky had actually cleared up some. The warm sunlight leaked down to hit my face as we walked. I smiled and took a deep breath of moist, mossy air, then looked back down at the ground just in time to notice and hop over a puddle of water on the trail.

I continued walking, paying more attention to where I was stepping, thinking that though it was pleasantly sunny, something felt slightly off. It then occurred to me that the woods were overly quiet. The usual ambiance of birdsong, and the scuffling of small creatures through the underbrush were completely absent. I stopped and scanned the area. Nothing moved. Lucy stopped a few feet ahead of me and looked back questioningly.

All of the tiny hairs on my body stood on end, as if my skin were charged with electricity. Lucy slowly turned to fully face me. She glanced around us, then noticing the eerie silence, her eyes widened. I nodded to the trail, signaling that we should continue walking. We started off again without a word, trying to step as lightly as possible. Instinct told me to stay as quiet as I could, like a rabbit trying to avoid a predator.

Suddenly a blue jay flew overhead, screeching out warning to all of the seemingly absent birds, then flew on away from us, leaving a weighted silence behind. My palms began to sweat. We walked for several minutes with only the sound of our footfalls and heavy breathing to let us know we hadn't gone deaf.

Lucy began darting nervous glances at me. I stopped again and gave her my full attention. She mouthed, "Should we run?"

I began to shake my head in reply, when suddenly there was a loud crack to the left and behind us, as if someone had stepped on a branch. We both froze, neither of us so much as breathing. Lucy kept her eyes on me, at a loss on what to do.

I scanned the woods around us, trying to spot the origin of the cracking sound, but the pine trees and other vegetation were too dense for us to see very far. All was still and silent again, but my instincts were screaming in my head for me to flee. I looked back to Lucy, nodded, and we broke into a full-blown run.

2

We ran through the woods, the trees a blur in my peripheral vision. After a short time I had to slow my pace for Lucy's shorter legs to catch up. Adrenaline pounded in my head like a second heartbeat. Lucy pushed harder and began to pick up speed, but then tripped and went flying to land in a heap on the moist soil. I skidded to a halt and crouched to grip her upper arms, dragging her to her feet. She brushed herself off and we continued running down the trail until the vegetation became less dense. We were almost safe. We slowed to a trot as we reached our street, then stopped in front of Lucy's house, both of us panting from the effort.

Lucy took a moment to catch her breath, then said, "Okay, that was weird, you felt it too right? Like someone watching us the whole way . . . the same someone who stepped on that branch."

I nodded my head and looked behind us, searching for a sign of our anonymous stalker. "What do you think it was?"

A shaky laugh erupted from Lucy.

I whipped my head back around to regard her. "What could you possibly be laughing about?" I asked, exasperated.

"Never mind, we're being ridiculous, it was probably just a deer or something." Despite her laughter, she didn't sound very sure. She looked away from my skeptical glare and began examining her palm, which had been scraped when she fell.

I continued to stare at Lucy until she finally raised her eyes back up to meet mine. She flinched slightly at my stubborn look. "C'mon Xoe, do you really think that we were being followed?"

I crossed my arms. "Yes, yes I do."

Lucy sighed. "By what? No one's seen any bears or mountain lions this close to town in years."

It was my turn to look down. "Maybe it wasn't a bear."

Lucy laughed again. "Who would want to follow us, and for what reason?"

I shrugged and met Lucy's eyes again, not able to brush the situation off as easily as she was. "I don't know, but we *were* followed."

Lucy put her hands on her hips. "Okay, say we were, what do we do about it now?"

I sighed. She had a point. "Nothing I guess." I managed a weak smile. "I'll see you tomorrow okay?"

With an uneasy nod and a wave goodbye, Lucy veered toward her house. I watched her go inside, then continued down the street.

My house wasn't far, and soon came into view. As I reached my door, I sensed movement in the woods to my right, but my eyes couldn't pick up anything out of the ordinary. That cracking sound we'd heard had *not* been a deer. A deer wasn't heavy enough to break a branch that large. I waited, pretending to examine the purple flowers that cascaded over the edges of the planter that rested to the side of my front door. Everything was still.

With a sigh, I unlocked my front door and entered my house, still feeling a little shaky. As soon as the door was shut, the tension in the middle of my back eased. I walked through the kitchen to the large dining room window and looked outside for . . . what? Feeling silly, I shook my head and went upstairs to my room.

Shutting the door behind me, I moved to the back left corner of my room that my queen size bed dominates. I sat on my forest green comforter and leaned against my mismatched yellow and blue pillows, feeling exhausted. I looked around my messy room, feeling numb, but also embarrassed for being so paranoid.

Like my mismatched bedding, there is no rhyme or reason to the decoration of my room. Besides my bed, the rest of the space is taken up by my desk, my clothes dresser, and my bookshelf. The empty wall space above my desk and dresser is consumed by posters from old horror movies. I'm a bit of a horror movie aficionado. I don't discriminate between old, new, hit movies, B movies, or anything in between.

My ancient, at least it seemed ancient to me, stereo system rested on the floor beside my desk. At any given time, my room is strewn with the cases of whatever CDs I'm obsessed with at the moment, plus a few books. On the other side of my desk is the door to my bathroom. That is one of the few positives about my room, my own private bathroom. The large picture window in the adjacent wall isn't bad either.

I reached down to where I had dropped my stuff and pulled my English book out of my backpack, then stood to set it on my desk. First day and we already had an assignment. It was just plain cruel. If I didn't do the homework now, I would procrastinate until the day it was due. My goal was to do a little better in school this year. The classes weren't exactly hard for me. It was more a lack of motivation that kept my grades down. There were just so many books that I wanted to read, and none of my school material made the cut.

I sat down at my desk, my mind still preoccupied, trying to come up with an explanation for the eerie experience in the woods. No matter how I tried to justify what had happened, I kept coming back to the same conclusion: someone or something had followed us, and he/she/it chased us when we ran. The thought briefly crossed my mind that predators will chase you if you run. It's instinct. They simply can't help themselves. I suppressed a shiver and stared at my English book for several minutes, then got up and went downstairs. Tomorrow, I'd do it tomorrow. Ri-ight.

My mom was getting home from work just as I reached the living room. She's a field biologist. I'm not sure exactly what she does, something to do with birds. I tried having her explain it to me once, but when she got to the part about collecting dead bird bodies to study, I decided I was okay with not really knowing what my mom does. Her job takes her out of town a lot, which can be good and bad. I miss her, but having free range of the house does *not* suck.

My mom noticed me and gave me a warm smile that reached her chocolate brown eyes. I get none of my looks from my mom. Her dark, wavy hair and tan skin are in sharp contrast to my blonde paleness. I probably look more like my dad, but I never knew him, so I have no proof.

My mom's hands were full with what looked like plastic bags of Chinese take-out. My stomach growled as the smell of greasy food hit me. We don't have the healthiest eating habits, not that I'm complaining. Our main dinners of choice are pizza and Chinese food. If we get bored we occasionally throw in some Indian or, gasp, have a home-cooked meal. On the rare occasion that we decided on home cooking, the task always fell to me. My mom and cooking apparatus of any kind just do not mix.

My mom took the bags to the rectangular, pale wood dining table, while I grabbed us each a glass of water. See, we're not *that* unhealthy, water is good for you. Plus there are usually vegetables in Chinese food. Don't judge us.

My mom pulled out a matching pale wood chair, smoothing the skirt of her burgundy cotton dress as she sat. I followed suit, then dug in the bags for the included wooden chopsticks, handing a set to my mom. We took the little cartons of food out of the bags and placed them between us on two woven yellow placemats. My mom watched me with curiosity in her dark eyes.

"How was your first day?" she asked casually.

"Eh," I replied, "same old, same old. I've got three classes with Allison, two with Lucy, and one with Brian, so that's good."

My mom smiled. "Any cute boys?"

Ugh. I sighed, "Must you always ask that question?"

My mom nodded enthusiastically. "Of course. It's a mom's duty."

I ignored her question and focused on my food.

"Any interesting classes this year?" she asked, taking my silence for the dismissal that it was.

"C'mon mom, are there ever any interesting classes in high school?"

She laughed her usual, full-throated laugh. "It could happen."

"When hell freezes over," I replied with a smile. "How was your day?"

"Same old, same old," she mimicked. "I may have to stay a few days in Washington next week."

I nodded and turned my attention back to my food. My mom prodded me a few more times about boys as we ate, but I unfortunately had to leave her disappointed. Once we finished eating, I headed back upstairs to my room.

As I walked in, I glanced at my English book sitting forlornly on my desk. I thought about trying to do my homework again for roughly two seconds, then grabbed the worn novel off the top of my dresser. I spent the rest of the evening re-reading *Galapagos,* by Kurt Vonnegut, until I was tired enough to go to sleep.

3

There was fire all around me. Everywhere I looked was a solid wall of flame, bright blue at the bottom fading into orange, then pale yellow. I should have been scared, or at least passing out from lack of oxygen, but I was somehow calm. I looked back at the wall of flame.

There were faces in the fire. Faces from my past and present, and some I didn't know. I saw my mom, Allison, and Lucy amongst them. The faces were all watching me, waiting to see what I would do. A large wolf appeared in the flames, its shaggy gray-black fur immune to the fire. He watched me with his head cocked.

I woke up drenched in sweat. I wiped my brow with the back of my hand as I recalled my dream. I'd had dreams of fire a lot in the past few months, some involving friends and family, and some where I was all alone. The wolf was new though. All of the dreams involved fire. The fire never burned me. I couldn't even feel the heat. I had no idea what they meant, or if they meant anything at all. The eerie part was that I always woke up with a fever that subsided after an hour or so.

I struggled out of the tangled mess I had made of my sheets and padded into my purple-themed bathroom, turning on the water in my marble tiled shower as soon as I entered so it would have time to heat up. Once the water began to steam, I added a little bit of cold to the mix, stripped off my still-damp t-shirt and boxers that I used as pajamas, and stepped in.

As the hot water washed over my face, I thought more about my recent slew of dreams. I couldn't understand being surrounded by fire, and not being afraid. I mean, I've never been particularly afraid of fire or anything, but I'm sure if I were surrounded by it in the waking world, I'd be more than a little scared.

My mom, who likes to interpret dreams, had quite a few theories, but none that really made sense to me. She told me that fire could symbolize change, life and death, re-growth, or a myriad of other things. It could be different for each person. I had no idea what fire was to me, but I knew there was more meaning to my dreams than simple interpretations could foretell. I've always had a strong sense of intuition. Something bad was coming. Hopefully our house wouldn't burn down.

My train of thought had led me to forget whether

or not I'd shampooed my hair yet, so I did it again, just in case. I'd been doing that a lot lately.

When I was done, I turned off the water and slid open the glass shower door. Steam seeped out into my small, but beloved, bathroom. I grabbed a fluffy purple towel from the wall rack and wrapped it around me, then moved to look into the round mirror above my sink, clearing a circle in the condensation with my palm. I wiped my moist hand on my towel and peered at my reflection.

I looked like I'd seen a ghost. My face was even paler than usual and I had dark circles under my bright green eyes. The row of big, round light bulbs above my mirror made the dark circles look severe. The dreams were not only weirding me out, they were interfering with me getting a good night's sleep . . . and causing me to run out of shampoo. Sighing, I ran a comb through my wet hair and left it at that. I dressed in jeans and a dark green t-shirt that emphasized my eyes, and went to school.

When I reached my Biology class, Allison didn't even bother to tell me her thoughts on my outfit of choice. She simply straightened her satiny burgundy tank-top that went with her designer jeans and dark-brown suede boots. It seemed Allison was beginning to view me as a lost cause. Okay by me.

Mrs. Sanders had decided that the second day of class was a perfect day for dissection. Earthworm guts in the morning. Yum. Mrs. Sanders waddled from table to table, letting us choose our sickly gray earthworms with long tweezers from an industrial size jar. .

"Why Xoe? Why *worms*?" Allison whined.

"Look at it this way Al, it could be way, way worse. In Advanced Bio they have to dissect cats and baby pigs," I said, turning Allison a lovely shade of green.

Allison was basically the worst lab partner in existence. She refused to touch anything slimy, stinky, or otherwise, even with gloves. I tried not to breathe in the odor as I pinned the poor departed earthworm to the blue foam inside the metal dissection tray. I then poised my scalpel to cut along his underside, following the diagram in our Biology books. Some sort of fluid squirted toward Allison as I punctured the worm, causing her to jump out of her chair and emit a girly scream. I practically fell over laughing, as did those seated near us. I hadn't squirted her on purpose, total accident. Scout's honor.

No one seemed to have much success with the worms. By the time class was reaching its end, most of the little creatures had been annihilated into unrecognizable bits of goo. The bell rang before anyone had cleaned his or her tray, so we all had to rush to do it before Ms. Sanders would let us leave. We were going be late for our next classes, with written excuses in hand. Things were looking up.

By the time lunch rolled around, I was still in a fairly good mood. That was, until Lucy and I walked together to the cafeteria to find that Dan was already at our table waiting for us. Lucy sat down right beside him, pretending she was doing nothing out of the ordinary. I considered for a moment sitting somewhere else, but then grudgingly sat down across from Dan and Lucy.

Dan scooted a little closer to Lucy as I sat, being horribly obvious. Lucy's pale green, lightweight sweater and khaki pants looked out of place against Dan's charcoal colored t-shirt and dark-wash jeans. Dan met my observant gaze almost territorially. My pulse sped up just a bit. What was with him?

Allison arrived with her lunch and sat down next to me, frowning at Dan and Lucy's closeness. I pulled my oh-so nutritious lunch, a granola bar, out of my backpack and started munching on it, maintaining eye contact with Dan defensively, trying to ignore the feeling of my hair standing on end. The granola felt like cardboard as it reached my stomach.

"Don't you have a lunch?" Dan asked Lucy, turning away from my glare.

"Oh, um, I forgot," Lucy answered.

Forgot? She never forgot. I had the sneaking suspicion that she simply didn't want to eat in front of Dan. I would never understand the way girls act around guys. Missing lunch just so he wouldn't see you eat? Sorry, but I wasn't missing lunch for anything short of Johnny Depp.

"Do you want me to get you something?" Dan

pressed, looking down at Lucy like she was a rare, delicate flower.

Lucy's skin darkened with a blush. She looked down at the table. "Oh, no thanks, I'm good." After a moment of silence, she quickly added, "Thank you for the offer though."

"You're really not hungry?" I prodded, annoyed with Lucy's behavior.

"No," she replied, her skin somehow going even darker.

"I can't remember the last time I saw you skip lunch," I went on. "It just seems kind of weird." Okay, so I was being cruel, but Dan's presence had me in a bad mood.

Brian trotted up to our table to squeeze in between Allison and me, saving Lucy from further prodding. He was wearing his football jersey and jeans, even though the green and yellow jerseys looked terrible on just about everyone. He set his lunch tray on the table and smiled mockingly when Allison looked down her nose at him.

Dan watched Brian like a hawk, scooting even closer to Lucy. Brian stared back at Dan, mouth screwed up in confusion, then his brow furrowed over his suddenly defensive glare. Uh oh, I could feel the testosterone rising. Dan and Brian continued to stare at each other. Dan was intimidating, and Brian, well, he tried. Something that sounded like a low growl trickled from Dan's throat. Brian blinked, the defensive look on his face slipping into one of confusion.

"Did you just growl at me?" Brian asked in disbelief.

Dan continued to stare. Brian frowned, but held his ground. What the heck was going on? I mean, it's not like masculinity contests are uncommon amongst teenage boys, but this was just plain odd. Lucy was practically cowering. Allison was looking back and forth between the two boys like they had just sprouted second heads.

"What is with you?" I asked Dan, exasperated.

He turned his icy glare to me, making me wish I hadn't spoken. Brian seemed relieved to have the attention off him.

Mustering up my courage, I raised my eyebrows. "Well?" I asked, a little more shakily than I would have liked.

Dan suddenly snapped out of it as a small smile crossed his face. Next he started laughing. "I totally had you guys going," he said, laughter tinting his words.

Brian laughed hesitantly and soon Allison and Lucy joined him, brushing off the awkward moment. I didn't get the joke.

The bell rang.

Brian slowly rose with his tray, eyes never leaving Dan. "I'll see you guys later."

Apparently Brian was unsure of the "joke" as well. I

watched Brian walk to the trashcan and dump his mostly uneaten food. Dan stayed seated, practically pressed against Lucy, until Brian was out of sight. He then insisted on walking Lucy to class. She seemed to be deciding between being pleased or maybe just a little creeped out. They walked out, leaving Allison and me alone.

"What on earth was that about?" Allison asked.

I raised my eyebrows at her. "I told you he was a creep."

Allison's brows knit together in confusion. "But he *growled* at Brian, like a dog or something. Was he seriously just kidding around?"

"I don't know, but I don't get the joke. Maybe we should cancel on Saturday."

Allison sighed. "I don't know if Lucy will go for it. Besides, he really could have just been joking."

"He sure has a weird sense of humor," I replied with a scowl.

Allison gave me a weak, humoring smile and we headed for gym. The rest of the day went by as usual, but Lucy and I had Allison give us a ride home, just in case.

The next few days of the school-week were uneventful. Dan sat with us at lunch, with no more shows of male dominance, joking or otherwise. He continued to stare at me during English, but never tried to speak to me alone again. When Friday finally came, the elation I usually felt at the weekend was tainted by the fact that Dan was still included in our Saturday plans.

Lucy and Allison had seemingly forgotten about his weird moment, or else they simply chose to ignore it. I, on the other hand, had not forgotten, and was dreading Saturday. In addition to the evidence I had suggesting that something was seriously wrong with Dan, I also just had an uneasy gut feeling about him. My intuition was still screaming that something bad was coming . . . or maybe it was already here.

4

Allison had decided that the shopping couldn't wait until next weekend, so we were going Friday afternoon. Lucy and I waited outside my house for Allison to come pick us up. Not that we couldn't drive, we both had our licenses, but sadly, no cars. Allison's parents bought her car for her on her 16th birthday.

Lucy and I were sitting on the swinging redwood and wrought iron bench that dominates the left side of my front porch, when Allison's dark blue Nissan *Sentra* pulled into my driveway. I matched Lucy's resigned sigh with one of my own. Neither of us enjoys shopping, but Allison has a tendency to beat at your resistance until you finally just give in to whatever she wants.

"You ready for this?" I asked Lucy.

Lucy nodded her head with a look of determination. "As ready as I'll ever be."

I stood and straightened my jeans and lightweight navy sweater, then turned to wave goodbye to my mom, who I could see through the kitchen window. Lucy and I strode toward Allison's car to meet our fate. I stole the front seat, forcing Lucy to slide into the back as we were assaulted by some generic girly pop music blasting from Allison's car speakers. I immediately grabbed the volume knob and turned the music down to a bearable (or at least as bearable as girly pop can be) volume.

"Remind me why we're friends with you?" I asked Allison playfully.

"It's because I have a car," she replied with a smile. She glanced back still smiling to acknowledge Lucy, but her smile slipped a little as she noticed Lucy's sweater, which was practically the twin of mine. Allison looked back at me, then at Lucy again. "What are you, the *Bobbsey Twins*?"

I sighed. "It wasn't on purpose, don't judge, you're not exactly looking your usual self today."

Allison looked down at her plain white t-shirt and torn, faded jeans. She shrugged. "Laundry day."

I smiled and said jokingly, "I knew there must be some valid excuse."

"Of course," Allison replied as she mimicked a royal bow with the top half of her body. She put the car in gear and began to maneuver out of my driveway. She glanced at me as we reached the road. "Did your mom give you any shopping money?"

"Yeah," I replied, "she was so shocked that I was actually going back-to-school shopping that I didn't even have to ask her, she just excitedly ran for her wallet." I held up my mom's gray and gold credit card as evidence.

"Lucy?" Allison asked, keeping her eyes on the road.

"Yep." Lucy's hand appeared between Allison and me, holding a fifty dollar bill.

Within a few minutes, we were driving past the Shelby cemetery. Cemeteries give me the creeps, especially the one in Shelby. Lucy and I visited it after Lucy's grandma passed away. We had walked among the rows of graves, all the way to the back where the oldest tombstones loomed, some of them dating back to the early 1800's. I could feel the age of the place, like the spirits of the long-dead corpses were surrounding me, trying to push me out. I know logically that ghosts don't exist, but the sudden feeling of panic that scraped across my skin while I was among the dead begged to differ.

Once the cemetery was out of sight, I let out a breath I hadn't known I'd been holding. I turned my attention back to the narrow road ahead of us. We soon approached what Shelby calls a "mall". It was more of a hallway according to Allison.

We parked in the partially full lot and stepped out

of the car to be met by a cool breeze. I wouldn't have minded hanging around outside for a bit, but I grudgingly followed Allison straight inside the mall to its fluorescent-lit corridor.

The mall was the stuff of nightmares. Salespeople called to us from little kiosks in the middle of the hallway, asking us what cell phone service we had or if we had ever heard of the *Dead Sea*. Groups of people from our high school were clustered together, laughing and ignoring the fact that they were totally clogging the sporadic flow of foot-traffic. Lucy and I followed Allison as she veered into one of the chaotic, brightly colored stores.

Allison got right to work, like a tiger on the prowl. Soon Lucy and I had piles of clothes draped over our arms. We trudged back to the fitting rooms before Allison could weigh us down with yet more clothing. The fitting room attendant was a petite woman, probably only about 5'1", with bright red, curly hair. She showed me to my own little stall and hung all of my clothes on the little hooks inside.

Once I was away from Allison's prying eyes, I picked through her selections for anything that I would actually wear. A miniskirt and a pale pink tank top went immediately into my discard pile. Next was a dark red, long-sleeved shirt made out of an almost sheer cotton. Surprised that Allison had actually chosen something I might wear, I tried it on.

The shirt made me look even more pale than usual,

but my green eyes were in sharp contrast, which I kind of liked. When I wore it to school, Allison would probably tell me that it was a bad color for me, then I could tell her that she had picked it out . . . totally worth it.

Along with the red shirt, I bought a new pair of jeans and a fitted, shiny dark brown leather jacket. The jacket was way more class than I was used to, but I figured my regular garb would help to dress it down. Lucy bought a red dress that I would never have guessed she would go for. Allison practically beamed.

We went to several more stores where Allison loaded Lucy and me up with more clothes, without losing an ounce of the same conviction she'd had in the first store. I was coerced into a few more clothing items, but ignored Allison's attempt to replace my beloved sneakers.

When the clothes shopping was finally finished, Allison insisted that we visit the makeup counter at one of the two larger department stores in the mall. Allison was drawn to the perfume counter like a moth to a flame, so I followed Lucy to browse all of the little sticks and squares of makeup.

Lucy held up two different tubes of lip-gloss in front of my face. "Which one do you think?"

Was she serious? I had never seen Lucy buy makeup before. She never expressed any sort of interest in it. "Um . . . " I replied, then quickly pointed to one of the tubes with my finger. "That one."

"You just randomly chose one, didn't you?"

I bit my lip. "Umm . . . yes."

Lucy smiled and shook her head at me, then called out, "Allison!"

Allison came trotting over with a little hot pink plastic bag that I assumed contained her new perfume. Upon observing Lucy's gloss dilemma, Allison turned Lucy back in the direction of the counter and started holding different glosses up against her face. Allison handed a peachy-pink tube back to me without a word. I apparently was to buy it. It was only six dollars so I decided not to argue. I could always just give it to my mom.

By the time Allison had finished with her, Lucy had two hands full of makeup. She shuffled to the counter to buy it all. I was beginning to have a sneaking suspicion that Lucy's new penchant for makeup had something to do with Dan. It worried me. I did *not* trust Dan to be with my best friend. I didn't trust Dan period.

After Lucy purchased her makeup, Allison finally announced that we were done. We left the hallway of horrors behind us and piled back into Allison's car to drive back to my house. Fifteen minutes later we came crashing through my front door, hands full of bags. Lucy and Allison headed straight up to my room so that Al could give Lucy a makeup tutorial. I paused to toss my new tube of lip-gloss to my mom, who was sitting on one of the couches in our living room watching TV.

"Thanks hon," she called as I started up the stairs.

When I got to my room, Allison had already spread all of Lucy's makeup out on the floor. There was a pile of plastic wrappers, which had once encased the little containers, lying discarded to the side. Lucy and Allison were sitting on the floor facing each other, so I sat down near them, forming an uneven triangle.

"What's this?" I asked holding up a fat pencil with a light gold, shimmery tip.

"Highlighter," Allison answered, keeping her attention on her job of applying eye shadow to Lucy's eyelids.

"For *what*?"

Allison grabbed the pencil from my hand and crooked her finger at me. "Come here and I'll show you."

I raised my hands in surrender and scooted a little further away. I watched as Allison continued to work on Lucy's eyes. I found out what the highlighter stick was for . . . kind of. It didn't seem to make much difference, at least to my *untrained* eye. Once Allison was finally finished, Lucy turned to face me.

"What do you think?" she asked me.

Allison had done a good job. You could tell that Lucy was wearing makeup, but it was understated enough that it wasn't the first thing you noticed about her face. "It's . . . different," I answered hesitantly.

"It's perfect," Allison corrected. She held up a mirror in front of Lucy's face.

Lucy's eyes widened. "Wow, Al, I have to hand it to you, you know what you're doing."

Allison turned a wicked grin to me. "Your turn."

I held my hand up to my ear, as if hearing something far away. "Oh, what's that? I think I hear my mom calling me. Just a sec mom!" I stood and ran for the door before Allison could grab me.

Allison and Lucy left later that afternoon to eat dinner with their families, and I sat in my room to sulk. Spending time with my friends had temporarily distracted me from the fact that we would see Dan tomorrow, but now it was all I could think about.

I sat with the portable phone beside me on the bed, debating on whether or not I should try to wiggle my way out of our plans. I hated admitting it, but I was afraid of Dan.

I sighed, then reached out a hand to push the phone away from me. I couldn't cancel. Lucy and Allison seemed to trust Dan. If something happened and I wasn't there . . . well, I'd never be able to forgive myself, and that's just for starters. I was going. Everything would be all right . . . Yeah, and pigs can fly.

5

By Saturday morning the feeling of dread was a hard knot in my stomach. I was sick with nerves that I didn't really know how to explain. That's a lie. About the lack of explanation I mean. I hadn't understood the bad feeling when I first met Dan, but I could explain it now. He was . . . different. Off. Not that different or off were necessarily bad things, but in Dan's case they definitely were.

I ran a brush through my hair and dressed mechanically in a black tank top, more holey jeans, and my ever-present sneakers. Allison would loooove it. I grabbed my new shiny brown leather jacket, just in case. The nights were starting to grow colder, warning us of winter, even though September had barely begun.

As I was heading downstairs, I heard a knock at the front door. I grabbed my satchel with my wallet and house keys as I trotted across the living room to answer it. Lucy was waiting in her new red dress and a pair of cute, funky brown boots that gave her a little more height. I hadn't seen her buy the boots on Friday, but I had avoided the shoe section like the plague, so that wasn't saying much. The outfit was a little dressy, well, okay, *a lot* dressy for Lucy's normal taste.

As soon as I beheld her garb I exclaimed, "I knew it! You bought all that stuff to impress Dan!"

She was even wearing her new makeup. Her almond shaped eyes were delicately lined in black, and her lips were freshly glossed. And was that perfume I smelled? Color me horrified.

I gave her a disapproving look.

Lucy's olive skin darkened with a blush. She turned and walked back toward the car where Allison waited, not saying a word.

Lucy wasn't getting off that easy. I shut and locked the door behind me, then quickly caught up to her side. "How can you like him? All he does is stare! And what about the weirdness at lunch the other day? I know you haven't forgotten about that. He's totally whacked," I hounded her.

"He's cute," she replied, "and he only stares at *you*, and that's probably because you treat him like he's some sort of freak. He's pretty normal once you actually talk to him, and the lunch thing was just a joke." Lucy glanced through the car window at Allison, patiently waiting in the driver's seat, then gave me a look that clearly stated *don't tell Allison.* She slipped into the backseat before I could say anything else.

Frowning, I opened the car door and took my usual place in the front. Allison took my grumpy look in stride and started the car. She was dressed up as well, but that wasn't out of the ordinary. She wore dark-wash jeans, a dark purple cami, and one of those fitted vest thingies that were apparently in style in a dark gray. Her suede booted foot pressed on the gas, and we were on our way. The theater wasn't far from my house, well, nothing in Shelby is really *far,* but my anxiety at the whole Dan situation made the ten minute drive seem like hours.

Dan was already waiting when we pulled up into the parking lot of the old, dreary theater. The theater was originally built with only three screens, but had been expanded to fit seven. Dan stood with his arms crossed, dressed in casual gray slacks and a black v-neck t-shirt, topped with his brown leather jacket. His near-black hair was styled to perfection, as always. He looked expensive, and dangerous, or maybe I was just projecting. He watched us approach with his pale blue eyes, seemingly at ease. I was feeling anything but at ease.

We reached where he was standing and stopped a short distance in front of him. We then proceeded to stand there in awkward silence. I looked to Lucy and Allison, but Lucy stayed looking down and shuffling her feet, while Allison smiled goofily at Dan. I was surprised to see that Dan looked slightly nervous himself. He usually seemed so macho and self-possessed. An abashed grin began to creep across his face. Could he get any more confusing?

I sighed and gestured my arms toward the theater. "Shall we?"

Everyone nodded and we were finally able to vacate the parking lot. We continued across the sidewalk, past outdoor posters of movies I would have loved to see, but knew we wouldn't end up with. Allison and Lucy's boots clicked on the pavement while I followed behind them in my quiet sneakers. Dan held the door for us as we went inside, then stood too close to me as we purchased tickets to a generic chick flick that was detailed on the least appealing poster.

Our movie was in *theater seven,* all the way at the end of the hall. The walk to the proper screening room seemed to take ages, as did the process of choosing seats. Lucy, Allison, and I would usually sit in the row directly behind the hand railing that cut the theater in half. That way we could put our feet up on the bar, and not worry about any tall people sitting in front of us to block the view.

I almost thought we'd end up with different seats as Lucy and Allison just stood in the aisle, waiting for Dan to move, but when he didn't choose either, I sat where I wanted and waited for everyone else to follow.

Lucy sat next to me, then came Dan, then Allison.

Lucy smiled a contented smile, while Allison looked less than happy. It seemed like Al had finally realized Lucy's intent in wearing her new outfit, and was none too happy for the competition. I was pretty sure that Lucy had won the competition before it even started, but for Allison, it ain't over 'till it's over.

We were early. The previews hadn't even started yet, and the silence was thick. Sighing, I nudged Lucy with my elbow. "I'm going to get some popcorn."

She nodded, not offering to go with me, so I climbed over the rail to go to the concession stand by myself.

"I'll join you," Dan announced, then hopped over the rail before I could protest.

Shaking my head, I walked out of the theater and toward the concession stand with Dan trailing slightly behind me. I was trying my hardest to ignore his presence, when he grabbed my arm from behind and spun me to face him. My heart skipped a beat. I looked at him, startled.

"What are you playing at?" he hissed.

"What are you talking about? Let me go!" I replied angrily, trying to pry my arm loose from his iron grip.

His blue eyes were very close, looking feral. His fingers squeezed my arm, hard enough to bruise. His hand was large enough to enclose my bicep entirely.

"Don't be stupid. I can smell you, just tell me," he snapped.

Smell me?

Taking in my puzzled expression, he hesitated, cocking his head to the side like he usually did when observing me. He gave me a crooked smile. "You don't know, do you?"

I kept the same stupid expression on my face, jaw slightly agape.

He laughed to himself and shook his head. "Um . . . never mind, forget I said anything." He continued chuckling.

I opened my mouth to argue, but he simply turned around and walked back toward our section of the theater, moving with a carefree skip to his step.

I stood, stunned, rubbing my arm where he had grabbed me. I stayed like that for several minutes, not sure what my reaction should be. I finally walked back into the movie without popcorn. I had lost my appetite. I climbed back over the bar and sat down, ignoring a puzzled look from Lucy. At least the previews had finally started.

I rubbed my arm again where Dan had grabbed me. Yep, there was definitely going to be a bruise. I gave Dan a dirty look that he didn't notice, then settled in to watch the movie. Once the movie started I tried to get into it, but ended up letting my mind wander. The feeling of dread was back in my stomach and my thoughts were dark. I was no longer simply creeped out, I was scared. I replayed my unnerving experience with Dan in my head, trying to puzzle out exactly what had happened.

By the time the movie ended I was no closer to coming up with an explanation. The credits began to roll and we all stood to leave the theater. After waiting behind the few shuffling people who had managed to reach the aisle before us, we finally made our way through and walked outside. The chilly breeze made me glad that I had brought my jacket. I slipped it on while only half listening as Lucy and Allison talked about the movie on the way back to Allison's car. I caught Lucy claiming that the movie was decent, once you got past the done-and-done-again plot . . . I hadn't noticed.

I walked a little ahead of our group, huddled in my jacket. I stopped and waited at Allison's car for everyone to catch up. I avoided Dan's gaze as they reached me and looked to Lucy instead. She had Dan's jacket draped over her shoulders.

Allison looked toward Dan and Lucy, then glanced at me. "Irvine's?" she asked the group.

Dan looked confused.

"It's a pizza parlor," Allison explained.

Dan nodded. "Yeah, we'll meet you there."

We? Dan gave a slight wave and walked away with Lucy tagging a short distance behind him.

"Where are you going?" I called after her.

"I'm riding with Dan. I'll see you guys there," Lucy replied nonchalantly as she looked over her shoulder at me. She paused at the worried look on my face, but quickly recovered and hurried after Dan.

I slid into the passenger seat of Allison's car with her already talking about Dan. " . . . . I can't believe Lucy snagged him. She has the best luck with guys . . . "

Allison prattled on about Dan as she started the car and pulled out of the parking lot, but I couldn't hear her as I became lost in my own thoughts. What was Dan's deal? What was *I* playing at? Why would he ask that? I shouldn't have let Lucy go with him. My original perception of him seemed to be holding true . . . he was a *creep.*

After we had been driving for a few minutes, Allison realized that I wasn't listening to her. She glanced at me with an annoyed expression. "Hello? Xoe? Are you listening?"

Snapping out of my thoughts, I answered, "Sorry Al, I just have a lot on my mind right now." I gave her my full attention.

"Like what?" she prompted, looking concerned as she watched the road in front of us.

"Um, Dan said something weird to me," I replied after a moment of hesitation.

Allison waited a few seconds, and then seeing that I wasn't going to elaborate questioned, "Well? What did he say?"

As a scowl formed on my face, I began to rant, "First, he stares at me *all* week in English, but never says a word. He talks to you guys like you're perfectly normal. Then he manhandles me in the theater, *demanding* to know what I'm up to!What is that supposed to mean!"

Perplexed, Allison asked, "What you're up to? I should think it quite obvious . . . you're up to being crazy. And what do you mean, *manhandled*?"

"He grabbed my arm and got in my face!"

Allison glanced worriedly at me, finally taking me seriously. "Did you provoke him or something?"

I gave her an outraged look.

Allison had the courtesy to look abashed as she turned her attention back to the road. "Sorry, stupid question. Shouldn't we just talk to him about it? Give him a chance to explain himself?"

I shook my head, my anger fading into confusion. "No, I don't think that's a good idea. Let's just keep an eye on him, okay?"

"I guess," Allison conceded, "though it's probably all just a misunderstanding."

Realizing that I still hadn't convinced her, I stared at Allison angrily.

Allison reached a red light and tried to stare me down.

I kept staring right back, jaw clenched stubbornly.

Allison sighed. "I'm sure he was just joking. As for the staring, I think it's all in your head. He just has a weird sense of humor." The light turned green and she hit the gas.

I tried a calmer approach. "I have a bad feeling Al, I've had it all week, I can't explain it, but I'm worried."

The concern returned to Allison's face. "We'll keep an eye on him Xoe, but I'm sure there's nothing to worry about."

Hardly placated, I sat silently with my arms crossed the rest of the ride to Irvine's.

We met Dan and Lucy in the parking lot and went inside the restaurant to order our pizza. The pizza at Irvine's isn't particularly good or anything, but it's where we always went. We didn't really have that many choices. Plus, Irvine's is relatively adult-free.

The pizza parlor was decorated kind of like a retro diner. Red vinyl stools surrounded the counter and an old-style jukebox with neon lights dominated the back corner of the restaurant.We grabbed a booth that kept to the red vinyl theme and waited. Lucy sat next to Dan, still wearing his coat, with her shoulder pressed against his arm. She looked tiny next to him, especially with the jacket engulfing her narrow shoulders. Everyone dutifully ignored the menacing glares I periodically aimed at Dan. The waitress came and went.

"Xoe?" Lucy asked eventually. I had spaced out from the conversation, as I tend to do.

"Huh?" I replied.

"I asked what your plans are for tomorrow," she continued. "I was thinking about hiking. We haven't gone up the trail behind your house in a while."

Dan looked back and forth between the two of us, as if taking in every detail.

"Oh, yeah, sounds good," I mumbled as the waitress arrived with our pizza.

She leaned much farther over the table than was necessary, drawing attention to her low-cut red blouse, and making eyes at Dan. Had all of the girls in town gone crazy? It was the only explanation. The smell of sausage and mushrooms wafted up from the pizza and my mood brightened a little. Food was always a sure-fire way to draw me out of my doldrums.

I looked up from the pizza to see that Lucy, Al, and ironically Dan (who was too rude to be polite) were all hesitating, not wanting to be the first one to grab a piece. Etiquette be damned, I dug right in, signaling to everyone else that the awkward moment could end. I chewed the mediocre pizza. Irvine's really wasn't the best pizza around, but I don't refuse pizza, average or otherwise.

I devoured two pieces while Lucy and Allison daintily nibbled on their first slices. Dan had taken one bite of his and left the rest abandoned on his plate. Creepier and creepier.

After we were all apparently done eating, we sat for another excruciating hour where I was forced to witness Al and Lucy fawning over Dan the entire time. By the time we finally decided to call it a night, I'd bitten my fingernails down to little nubs. Lucy rode with Dan again with a promise to call me tomorrow.

As soon as Allison dropped me off, I rushed inside to call Lucy, then realized that she might not be home yet, considering that maybe Dan didn't speed like a maniac as Allison did. I decided to give her an extra fifteen minutes. I sat on the love seat in my living room, drumming my fingers on a throw pillow in my lap, then after precisely 13.5 minutes I dialed Lucy's number, letting it ring until the machine picked up. I hung up and waited another five minutes and called again.

"Hello?" Lucy's voice buzzed back at me.

I let out a breath of relief. "Lucy? Are you okay? I shouldn't have let you go alone with Dan. There's something wrong with him. He said the weirdest thing to me . . . "

"Xoe," she buzzed back, interrupting me, "something weird happened."

I paused, waiting for her to continue. The dread was back full swing. I switched the phone to my other hand so I could wipe the sweat off my palm onto my jeans.

Lucy continued, "He walked me to the front door, then he leaned toward me. I thought he was going to kiss me, you know? Then I felt a sharp pain in my arm and realized . . . he *scratched* me."

Shocked, I questioned, "What? Like took his nails and raked you?"

I heard Lucy sigh on the other end of the line. "Xoe, it's going to sound crazy, but, well, his hand looked different . . . kind of like he had claws."

A moment of stunned silence passed.

"Claws?"

"Yeah," she said. "Or maybe it was just the dim lighting. I keep second guessing what I saw, but the proof is on my arm."

"Is this some kind of joke?" I was getting angry. I hated jokes like this. I'm the most skeptical person I know, so they never worked. All anyone ever succeeded in doing was making me mad. Though that didn't explain why my heart was caught in my throat.

"It's not a joke Xoe," Lucy replied, tears straining her voice.

"Seriously?"

"Seriously."

"Stay right there Lucy, I'm coming over," I ordered.

"No, yo-ou can't, my parents will be home any minute." Lucy replied, hiccuping on her words. "I d-don't know what to do," she continued. "I'm scared Xoe. W-what if he comes back?"

I considered storming into her house anyway, but knew her parents would just send me back home. "Maybe you should call the cops and report the attack."

"And tell them what?" Lucy asked. "That m-my date scratched me, then politely went home?" She was getting louder as she spoke, edging on hysteria.

I felt numb, and wasn't quite sure what to say. "He just . . . left?" I asked finally.

"Yeah." She had suddenly roped in her sobs, regaining some of her composure. The fact that she had broken down at all was unnerving. Lucy never broke down. "I just stood there like a moron and watched him go."

I sighed. "What should we do?"

"What can we do?" she replied quickly. "I can't call the cops, I can't do anything. I don't understand what's going on." Lucy paused and I heard voices in the background. "My parents just got home, they'll want me to get off the phone . . . I have to go. Keep the phone near you okay? Just in case. I'll come over in the morning."

"Have your mom drive you," I ordered.

"Okay."

I heard the phone click as she returned it to its cradle. I sat unmoving, except for drumming my fingers on the table . . . yeah, I could already tell that sleep would not come easy tonight.

I paced back and forth across the living room. My thoughts were racing a million miles per minute. Lucy's story should have been hard to believe, but for some reason I didn't think she was imagining things. It explained the bad feeling I had about Dan, and all of his weird behavior . . . kind of.

I went upstairs and tried to go to bed, but it was no use. I got up and sat at my desk, turning on my computer. Once it was on I stared at it, not really knowing what I had intended to do with it. Look up cases of people scratching other people? Somehow I didn't think I would get much useful information from a search like that. I turned the computer back off and started pacing across my room. I hated inaction. I needed something proactive to do about the Dan situation, but I couldn't think of a thing.

I went back downstairs to the living room and turned on the TV. The volume blared and I hurried to turn it down before it woke up my mom. She had gone to bed early since she had to wake up at 6:00 am for an early hike with one of her friends. I started flipping through the channels and stopped on what looked like a relatively high-budget, black-and-white horror movie on *AMC*.

A woman was running terrified through the woods. She kept looking back at whatever was chasing her, like they always do in horror movies. The camera panned back to a man in tattered clothing, presumably the woman's pursuer. He paused on a hilltop framed by the full moon and turned into a . . .

My heart caught in my throat. It made sense, if I was willing to overlook the plausibility of it. All of Dan's behavior: growling at Brian, cocking his head like a dog all of the time, saying he smelled me . . . scratching Lucy. Dan was a *werewolf*.

I sat for a moment, stunned, then laughed at myself. A werewolf? Werewolves weren't real. They were the stuff of myth and legend. I ruefully shook my head and switched off the TV. Sleep. Sleep was what I needed. I rose from the sofa in deep consternation, and made my way back upstairs. I plopped down on my bed and stared at the ceiling. Maybe Dan just *thought* he was a werewolf. While I couldn't quite believe that he was a supernatural being, I could easily believe that he was mentally unstable.

What seemed like an eternity later, I finally dozed off. I dreamed that I was on fire, but not burning. Everything around me burned, my room, my house, and distantly I knew that my mom and my friends were burning too. I could hear their screams, but I just stood there watching the flames. A wolf howled.

6

I woke to knocking on my bedroom door. My t-shirt and boxers that substituted for pajamas were once again damp with sweat from my vivid dreams.

"Xoe? It's me, Lucy . . . your mom let me in," a timid voice called from the other side of the door.

I sprung from my bed and rushed to the door, stumbling over a book on the floor, still only half-awake. Did I mention I'm not a morning person? I opened the door to find Lucy waiting on the other side. She was dressed down in a dark brown t-shirt, even darker suede jacket, worn jeans, and hiking boots. I faced her and tried to remain calm—that is until Lucy shrugged off her jacket to bare her upper arm.

"He mutilated you!" I exclaimed, examining the scratches on her arm.

"It's not that bad," she replied calmly, "but look at

them, do they look like the work of human fingernails to you?"

As a matter of fact, they didn't. Four long, thin gashes marred her arm, deep enough to make me feel a little queasy at the sight. No, definitely not normal fingernails. I gingerly touched the area around the scratches. Her skin was burning hot.

I frowned. "Do you think you need stitches?"

Lucy shook her head. "I thought about it, but what would I tell the doctor?"

Good point. Lucy was trying to be calm, but her wide eyes gave her away. She was freaked. The dark circles under her eyes alluded to a sleepless night, and I didn't blame her. I wouldn't have been able to sleep either. I nodded and stood aside for Lucy to come into my room.

At the sound of footsteps, Lucy quickly shrugged back into her jacket. A few seconds later, my mom came around the corner from the stairway, dressed in a casual, gauzy green dress and flip-flops.

At the sight of Lucy my mom's face erupted into a smile that reached her warm brown eyes. "Have you had breakfast yet, Lucy?" she asked. "Our weekend breakfasts usually occur around noon, but we could make it a little earlier. It's been a while since I've seen you."

"No thanks," Lucy mumbled.

Taking in our expressions, a look of concern flashed across my mom's face. She pressed the back of her hand against Lucy's forehead. "Are you feeling okay, Lucy? You feel a little warm."

Lucy looked down at the floor, muttering that she was fine.

My mom looked back and forth between us, a frown creasing her brow. She reached up and felt my forehead. "You feel warm too honey, another dream?"

"Um, yeah, we'll talk about it later, 'kay?" I looked pleadingly at my mom. I hadn't told Lucy or Allison about my dreams.

She hesitated, but decided to let it go and headed back downstairs.

As soon as my mom was gone, we went into my bedroom and I shut the door. I continued into the adjoining bathroom and quickly brushed my teeth and washed my face, pulled on some jeans and a purple tank top, and went back into my bedroom barefoot to question Lucy.

"What dreams?" Lucy asked.

Sigh. Thanks a lot mom. "Um, I've just been having some weird dreams lately, nothing major."

"Please Xoe, I could use the distraction,"

I let out a loud breath. "For the past few months I've been having these *dreams*. I'm always surrounded by fire in some way, but I'm never scared. It's the weirdest feeling, almost peaceful."

Lucy studied my face, not understanding the significance. "What makes them different than any other dreams? I know you're not one to get freaked out by nightmares."

I looked down. "I don't know. They're just . . . different, and when I wake up I always have a fever."

"A fever? I guess that *is* kind of weird," Lucy conceded. "Why didn't you tell me sooner?"

"I just didn't think it was relevant," I replied. "Plus, I'm weirded out by them enough. I don't need to weird everyone else out too." I was feeling embarrassed and went for a subject change. "But now back to you, I think you have the more pressing matter."

"Yeah, yeah I guess I do," she mumbled.

"So what are our theories?" I asked her.

"Theories?" she replied, confused.

"Yeah," I answered, "those scratches are anything but normal, which means Dan probably isn't so normal either. Yesterday he told me he smelled me, and I *don't* stink. Now he's gone and scratched you, so I think there really is only one plausible theory. It's a little far-fetched I admit, but I've been thinking about it all night and it was all I could come up with."

Lucy just stared at me, a little green in the face.

"He thinks he's a werewolf," I stated matter-of-factly. I decided to leave out the fact that my idea came from a movie. I didn't want to make my theory less plausible . . . if that was even possible.

Lucy laughed in a less than convincing manner, but didn't reply.

"Do you have any better ideas?" I asked, feeling slightly offended.

Lucy shook her head. "It's not that Xoe, it's just . . . I think he actually *is* a werewolf."

I blinked slowly at her as I tried to figure out whether or not she was joking. "Come again?"

Lucy continued unperturbed, "Just think about it Xoe, what else makes sense? What has superhuman smell and claws? I'm not imagining it. His hand was *not* a human hand."

"I don't know what makes sense!" I practically shouted. "But Dan being a werewolf sure doesn't! You have been watching *too* many horror movies. Werewolves don't exist."

"I know what I saw!" she shouted back.

"Look," I replied, calmly as she began to cry, "It's pretty far out there, but maybe you're right. I know you wouldn't make it up."

I thought about what Lucy had said. I knew she wouldn't make something like that up, but people's eyes play tricks on them all of the time. It wouldn't help for me to point that out to her though. "He does act kind of . . . dog-like," I offered.

Lucy sat on my bed, defeated. She sat that way for several minutes.

I waited while we both processed the implications.

Lucy shook her head. "I don't know Xoe. I understand why you don't believe me. I can hardly believe myself, but I know what I saw."

I grabbed Lucy's arm and gently pulled her to her feet. "Let's take a walk. We'll try to come up with some alternative theories."

The only problem was, that having considered the alternatives, I knew there weren't any. I mean, the best I could come up with was that Dan *thought* he was a werewolf, could I fault Lucy for thinking that he really was one? Who was I to say that such things didn't exist? The legends had to come from somewhere.

The problem was that the only information I had came from movies, and the werewolves, according to the films, were always different. Some could only be killed by silver bullets, and others would die if you just whacked 'em with a big stick enough times. Some just changed once a month, on the night of the full moon, others changed the whole week of the full moon, and others could change at will. We needed answers, and answers we did not have. I guess we'd find out if Lucy's crazy theory was not so crazy after all once the full moon rolled around.

I moved my grip from Lucy's arm and took her trembling hand to lead her downstairs. The truth was what it was, even if big and growly.

7

I stopped by my back door to slip on my hiking boots and a jean jacket on our way outside. We journeyed out across my backyard together, then headed into the woods where Lucy and I had met so many years ago. We reached a damp, narrow trail that led through the tall pine trees to the wider, more used trail that connected to a different road. Running water sounded from a stream in the distance. It sounded close, but in reality, it was about two miles away. A cool breeze was blowing, scented with the autumn leaves.

Lucy fell in step behind me, seemingly lost in thought. Usually walking out in the woods was peaceful, but I could almost taste the tension emanating from Lucy. I glanced back at her a couple of times, but waited for her to talk first. She needed time to process things. She was so quiet that if not for the sound of her footfalls, I wouldn't have known that she was there. We walked for a good ten minutes that way, her trailing behind me, neither of us saying a word.

Lucy's voice finally cracked the silence. "Do you think I'm going to be a werewolf now? I mean, if that's what Dan is . . ."

So we were going with the werewolf theory then. That she took it so seriously made it seem more real to me, which I wasn't exactly grateful for. "I don't know," I answered honestly over my shoulder, "but whatever happens, we'll get through it, even if I have to lock you in a cage once a month."

Lucy quickened her stride to walk beside me. "A cage?" she asked.

I glanced at her. "Well, maybe not a cage," I replied, "though I don't know what else to use. We could just lock you in a room, but seeing as neither of us knows anything about werewolves, or whether or not Dan is one, I'd say better safe than sorry."

Lucy thought for a moment, then responded, "A cage it is then."

"We'll get online and do some research tonight. We of course won't find any solid answers, but knowing all of the legends can't hurt."

"Xoe," Lucy began slowly. "When I first thought of the werewolf thing, I freaked out and looked up the date of the full moon. It's tomorrow."

My mouth went dry. "I guess we'll need to find a cage sooner rather than later?" I asked half-heartedly.

We stopped walking and sat on a felled tree on the side of the trail.

"Do you think we should tell Allison?" Lucy asked, changing the subject.

I smiled. "She might not believe us." At Lucy's expression I corrected, "Okay, she definitely won't believe us. Though, I guess she'd have to at least consider it if you showed her the scratches."

"I don't know," Lucy countered. "She may not believe it even then. I'm still not sure I do."

I frowned. "Even if we tried to keep it quiet, she can always tell when we're trying to hide something from her. Remember the incident of the ruined shoes?"

Lucy gave a small smile. "How could I forget?"

I smiled back. "If she asks, we'll tell her, and she can decide for herself whether to believe us or not."

Lucy nodded as the smile slipped from her face.

I felt my smile slip too as I looked down at the ground. There wasn't much more to say, so we sat in melancholy silence. I could feel the moisture from the tree trunk seeping through my jeans, making me cold. I focused on scratching a patch of lichen off of a nearby rock, rather than thinking too hard on our problem. Little green flakes fell to the damp earth as I picked away.

I needed to put on a brave face for Lucy. I had a feeling that my calmness was the last thing holding her together. If I were her, I'd be falling apart right about now. I was near to falling apart as it was.

Finally, we got up and continued walking farther into the woods. Usually I would have brought my backpack with water, first aid kit, and pepper spray if we were going any sort of distance, but I guess my mind had been too preoccupied to remember when we left my house. It was stupid of me. You never know what might happen.

We had both been watching the ground in front of us for several minutes when Lucy turned her attention to the trail ahead. She paused with instant fear at what she saw.

8

I looked up to see what had stopped her. Dan was waiting expectantly farther up the trail. He was dressed in a green t-shirt, jeans, and his brown leather jacket, his hair styled to its usual perfection. He didn't make a move toward us. He just stood there and stared.

My heart sped as I wiped sweaty palms on my jeans. "W-what do you want?" I stammered loudly, backing up.

He just stood there watching us, then began to come forward.

I shouted, "Don't come any closer or I'll—" I blinked and he was only a few feet away. How had he moved so fast?

"Or you'll what?" he interrupted.

The next thing I knew he shoved me, then I was on the ground, looking at the branches above me, blue sky shining through. My vision swam, then darkness swallowed the branches whole.

I WOKE to deep blue eyes worriedly looking into my groggy green ones, and realized someone was shaking me. I scuttled backwards out of my assailant's grasp like a demented crab to take in the stranger who had been hovering over me.

Tousled deep brown hair, and a scruffy yet handsome male face went with the dark blue eyes that had been above me. He had a narrow, sweeping nose and his eyes were lined by a dark splash of lashes. Only his strong, sharp jaw and several days worth of stubble saved his face from femininity. He was about 6'1" with a, might I say, rather nice physique; lean, yet muscled. He wore a dark green sweater, worn jeans, and dark brown hiking boots that had definitely seen better days.

He tried to hide a laugh at my frenzied scuttle, and I was too freaked to get mad. There was still the question of why I had been on the ground, unconscious in the woods with only this handsome stranger to blame. It was only when I saw Lucy standing behind the stranger unharmed, that I was able to stuff my heart back down my throat.

They both watched and waited for me to talk.

Something tickled at the edge of my memory. "Dan! Where'd he go?" I shrieked. I remembered Dan attacking us now, well, I remembered him attacking me, before I lost consciousness.

Lucy shuffled forward, pale and wide-eyed. Her jeans were dirty and her soiled jacket was torn at the elbow. "Dan pushed you down. I tried to run toward you, but suddenly he had me on the ground too. He was so fast Xoe. I tried to struggle, but he pressed me down until I couldn't move. He said I had to come with him.He said I would be . . . dangerous." Lucy paused as she glanced at the stranger, then quickly went on, "The next thing I knew, Jason was there, tearing him off me." Tears began to well in Lucy's already puffy eyes.

I dizzily stumbled to my feet, then grabbed Lucy in a hug, feeling pine needles in her hair. "Where did he go?"

"I-I don't know," Lucy said.

I pulled away from Lucy and turned to this so-called Jason character. "Where did he go?" I asked more confidently. "I can't believe he just gave up that easily."

Jason studied me for a moment, as if considering which answer would upset me the least, then shrugged, apparently deciding on no answer at all.

"You were the only one vertical at the time. You had to see him leave," I pressed.

He shrugged again. "My attention was on making sure that the two of you were unharmed. I did not see where he went."

"So you were completely unconcerned with the

stranger that you found in the woods attacking two people?"

Shrugging again, he smirked and walked up to grab my arm. "I will walk you girls home."

I ripped my arm away from him and got in his face. "We need the truth. Something weird is going on and it is just *way* too convenient that you were there at just the right time. No offense, but Dan is bigger than you, and I don't think he would exactly run screaming at the sight of you. Your story don't wash pal."

He reached out brushed back a strand of my hair that had fallen into my eyes. I jerked away, startled.

He chuckled at my reaction.

I pointed my finger a few inches away from his face. "Now, is *so* not the time to mess with me."

He smiled. "I can see that, but we do need to get you both home. It's not safe out here."

I grabbed Lucy and stormed back down the trail, with Jason following a short way behind us. Though Lucy had stopped crying, she was leaning heavily on me as if she'd fall without my support. We stumbled on as Jason caught up to walk on my other side. I focused on the trail, trying to hide the fact that my heart was thundering in my ears.

"I spoke the truth," he said. "I don't know why he fled. Do you know him?"

Sighing, I answered a bit more breathily than I would have liked, "Yeah, we know him . . . unfortunately."

I walked a little faster, trying to end the conversation.

Jason simply matched my stride and pressed on. "Have you spent much time with him?"

I frowned at him, almost tripping on a stone. I had to pause for a moment and get a better grip on Lucy. "I thought you were just the 'innocent bystander', not involved in the situation, so why do you care?"

Jason thought for a moment, then shrugged again. "Just making conversation," he said, effectively ending the conversation.

By the time we arrived at my house, Lucy had somewhat regained her composure, though her normally self-assured eyes still had haunted shadows chasing across them.

I put my hand on her back in a comforting gesture. She was trembling ever so slightly; a frightened mouse came to mind. I pushed Lucy in through the back door and turned to Jason. "There's something weird about your story, well okay, a whole lotta somethings. You know more about Dan than you're letting on. I trust you as much as I trust him. Stay away from Lucy."

That carefree smirk returned to his face, but within a moment wiped clean to leave his expression all stony-serious. His deep blue eyes looked angry. "Stay out of the woods, and stay away from Dan. He *is* dangerous," he warned, holding my gaze to make sure I understood.

"Thanks, but tell me something I *don't* know," I

replied, then slammed the door in his face. So maybe he didn't deserve my temper, but then again, maybe he did.

I walked up to my room to find Lucy already sitting on my bed, staring blankly at a framed picture of her, Allison, and me, standing together with large grins on our faces. We'd taken it over the summer by Allison's pool. The summer seemed very far away.

Realizing my presence, she looked up and asked, "Can I stay over tonight, Xoe?" Her eyes pleaded with me.

I knew my mom wouldn't mind Lucy staying over on a Sunday, but Lucy's strict parents were a whole other story. "You're welcome to, if you can convince your parents."

Lucy gave me a small smile. "They left for Portland to visit my uncle this morning, remember? They would actually prefer it if I stayed here. My sister is staying at a friend's house too."

Well that settled that.

My mom, as expected had no problem with Lucy staying over. She ordered us a pizza and the three of us sat in the living room with the pizza box on the coffee table. I grabbed my first slice and began to wolf (no pun intended) it down. Lucy's first piece sat forlornly on her paper plate.

My mom watched Lucy carefully. "Not hungry?"

Lucy looked up from her plate, startled. "Oh, um, no, not really hungry."

My mom patiently waited for Lucy to elaborate.

I tried to distract her. "When are you leaving for Washington, mom?"

My mom glanced at me for a moment. "Probably Wednesday." She turned her attention back to Lucy. "Besides your hike, you've been here all day. I haven't seen you eat."

Lucy pushed her plate a little farther away from her. "My stomach has been upset lately."

My mom nodded and seemed to settle for Lucy's answer, but I caught her glancing at Lucy skeptically out of the corner of her eye for the rest of the evening.

When all that was left was a cheese-soaked box, we headed back to my room. Lucy borrowed one of my t-shirts and some plaid pajama pants to sleep in. While she got ready for bed in my bathroom (she stayed over enough to warrant her own toiletries kit), I toured around the house and made sure the doors and all of the windows were locked. Paranoid, who me?

I paused as I passed the hall mirror. I looked at my reflection numbly. Things hadn't really set in yet. I felt as if I were walking in a dream. I lightly touched the carved wood frame of the mirror, half expecting it to disappear, just a fragment of this horrible dream. Firm, solid wood pressed beneath my fingertips.

I returned to my room to find Lucy staring blankly from her perch on my bed. I spared her a final worried glance then took my turn in the bathroom. By the time I was finished brushing my teeth and picking stray pine needles out of my hair that I hadn't noticed until then, Lucy was curled up into a ball on my bed, fast asleep.

I crawled into bed next to her and stared at the ceiling. In my head, I reviewed all of the events of the weekend. Reason told me to assume that Jason was in league with Dan, but my gut was inexplicably arguing against that possibility. I instantly wanted to trust him, just like I instantly wanted to distrust Dan.

I finally fell asleep to visions of werewolves dancing in my head.

9

L ucy seemed to be feeling a little more steady in the morning. We each took our turns in the shower and I let her borrow some of my clothes. She had to cuff the jeans a few times, but the long-sleeved, navy cotton shirt fit her pretty well. Hoorah for the bustily-challenged. I dressed in my usual theme: jeans, dark blue v-neck t-shirt, and my ubiquitous sneakers.

We ran downstairs and grabbed granola bars for breakfast. I filled my travel mug with coffee from the pot my mom, saint that she is, had made. I added a small amount of creamer and pushed the lid onto my mug, making that moist suction noise that travel mugs tend to make. I glanced at the clock to see that it was already 7:15. We rushed out the door to fast-walk to school.

Our silence was weighted with fear and worry.

Neither of us wanted to be the one to break it. I think we both were all too aware that the full moon was fast approaching. Tonight we would have answers, or at least one answer. So much was still unexplained.

Lucy's timid voice cracked the silence. "So, um, if we're right about Dan, what are we going to do? I mean, if I'm to believe that werewolves exist, then it would also stand to reason that some of the legends about them exist . . . " She stared at the ground, refusing to meet my eyes.

"We'll think of something. I won't let you go through this alone, even if your theory is right, and I'm starting to think it is. Why else would Dan say that you would be dangerous?" I asked.

"I know," Lucy said. "I've been thinking about that too."

I hesitated on my next question, not sure if I would make things worse by asking. "Are you scared?"

Lucy stopped walking and met my eyes. "Terrified."

I kept my gaze locked on hers until she looked back down and began walking again. I followed shortly behind her. The ensuing silence was no less strained. We arrived at school just as the first bell rang, and we parted to go to our respective classes. I reached biology and slid into my seat next to Allison just as the second bell rang. I was unable to concentrate on the lecture, which was nothing new, but this time it was more than my short attention span standing in my way.

Once class was over, I met with Lucy before second

period. We sat in our usual seats in the front, but Lucy was so obviously not her usual self. She kept her eyes on her desk and did not raise her hand to answer one single question. I guess I couldn't blame her. The teacher darted a few concerned glances at Lucy, but apparently decided to leave her alone. Lucy didn't seem to notice.

At lunch Lucy and I waited at our table, both of us deep in thought. Neither of us had remembered to grab lunch as we rushed out the door that morning.

"What's with you two today?" Allison questioned as she sat down in her slim-fit jeans and pink button-up blouse with her purchased lunch. "You both look like you've seen a ghost."

I looked up and forced myself to smile. "There's nothing wrong, we're fine."

Lucy nodded her head in agreement. "We're fine."

Our denials did nothing to placate her. Allison pressed on, "Out with it. The two of you are hiding something and you are going to tell me what it is right this instant."

Well, when she put it that way . . . I started from the beginning.

By the time I had finished filling Allison in on the events she had missed over the weekend, she was staring at me in stunned silence. "You're kidding," she sputtered. "I don't get the joke guys, what's the punch line?" She looked back and forth between the two of us, eyebrows raised.

"No punch line." I replied as Lucy lifted her sleeve to expose her scratches as evidence.

Allison grabbed Lucy's arm and thoroughly examined the scratches. Lips pursed, Allison took a moment to consider the unlikely situation. "This is so not funny," Allison said finally.

I gave her a blank look.

Allison looked back and forth between Lucy and me. "C'mon guys," Allison pleaded, "joke's over."

I sighed, "No joke, no punch line. We're not entirely sure about our conclusion yet, but ... "

Allison snorted loudly. "I simply cannot believe that Lucy is going to," then she lowered her voice, "turn into a werewolf tonight, but I suppose I can afford to humor you two. If this turns out to be some elaborate prank, I will not be pleased."

"Humor us all you want Al. I'd love it if this were a joke. We'll all find out tonight," I said tiredly.

"So what then? We'll just tie Lucy up and wait out the full moon?" Allison asked.

Now it was Lucy's and my turn for stunned silence.

"Well?" Allison questioned raising her eyebrows, "Do either of you have a better idea?"

Lucy looked at me.

Shrugging I turned to Allison. "My place or yours?"

Allison snorted, then we all huddled together to discuss our plans. I felt better having Allison involved, and I could tell that Lucy did as well. Three heads were better than two.

Once everything was settled, we just had to wait out three more classes. Then we would set our sorta-plan into action. We would all go together to the local hardware store to try and find some sort of restraints, then we would wait at my house until the sun started to go down.

We discussed just waiting for the full moon at my house, but I wasn't about to put my mom in danger of being eaten or whatever it is that werewolves do. In the end, we decided that we would tell my mom we were going to Allison's, but instead we would drive out into the woods to tie Lucy up and see what happened.

Our plan was awful at best, and I was anxious to get it over with. Considering Lucy's possible fate, and what might happen to Allison and me should our restraints fail, wasting our time in class seemed all too pointless. At least, I thought it did. Lucy refused to miss class, even under the extreme circumstances.

For the first time in my life, gym went by painstakingly slow. Not even dodge ball could distract me from the ever-ticking clock. I walked into English, ready to count the minutes, and my heart skipped a beat. Dan was in class.

"You have some nerve!" I stormed up to him. "I can't believe you're showing your face around here! I'm going to . . ."

"Xoe!" Ms. Masterson thundered. "Sit down right this minute! What's wrong with you?"

I plunked down into my chair, sparing a mutinous

glare for Ms. Masterson's turned back. Dan chuckled. Chuckled! I could barely contain my fury. Brian gave me a concerned glance from his spot on the other side of me. I sat and fumed, clenching the sides of my desk, white-knuckled. My face felt afire. My anger was a palpable thing.

Dismissing my outburst, Ms. Masterson had barely begun her lecture, when the classroom door opened and interrupted her. And who should walk in but Jason, our supposedly valiant rescuer, dressed in a red flannel shirt and faded jeans. This *had* to be a dream. I mean c'mon. He took the empty seat behind me while Ms. Masterson glared at him. Jason's appearance had cooled my anger by a few degrees, replacing it with confusion.

I stared at Dan. He ignored me, a small, infuriating smile on his face. I could feel Jason's eyes on us. After what seemed like a lifetime of me staring at Dan, Brian glancing worriedly at me, and Jason watching all three of us—the bell finally rang.

Dan stood quickly and rushed out the door. I was blocked from him by the other students shuffling out of the classroom. By the time I pushed past everyone and reached the hall he was nowhere to be found. I felt stupid for not having predicted his escape. I really hadn't thought he'd run. I whirled on Jason, who was walking out of the classroom behind me.

Hands on hips, I stared up into his dark blue eyes, just now noticing his clean-shaven face and less scruffy appearance, though his hair was still a tousled mess. Hmm, he did have a nice smile . . . wait. I mentally slapped myself for getting distracted,

I crossed my arms, put on a stern face, and took on a bad Cuban accent. "Jaaason, you got some 'splainin to do." I still wasn't buying the story he'd given us yesterday, now more than ever. He knew more about Dan than he had let on and he was going to tell me what that was.

"Skip sixth period," he replied with a smile. "Let's take a walk."

I nodded, ignoring the risks. What was the worst that could happen?

Don't answer that.

Avoiding the not-so-watchful security guards, we slipped outside and began our walk. A surprise gust of chilly air blew my hair back from my face as we went. I glanced up at the sky as we walked off school grounds to see ominous clouds promising yet more rain. The smell of ozone was thick in the air. Joy.

"I think that Lucy may be in trouble," Jason began.

"Tell me about it," I replied. "Dan *scratched* her. We have some theories, but the most prominent one means that Lucy's 'trouble' will start tonight, and I think you know something about it." I stopped walking and looked at him expectantly.

A bitter smile crept across his face, doing nothing to mar his handsomeness . . . not that I noticed or anything. "You are correct," Jason confirmed. "Dan is indeed a werewolf, and Lucy will likely become one too. Now the question is, what are we going to do about it?"

My jaw dropped. I hadn't expected him to confirm everything I'd just said. He said *werewolf* like the word didn't hold a world of implications.

"Yep," I replied weakly as I started walking again, still feeling shocked and unsure. "That's the $10,000 question. So far we've come up with tying her to a tree in the woods."

Jason stumbled at my words, shock plain on his face. He recovered quickly, running his hands through his messy, dark brown hair. "Um, only if you are going to tie her up with silver chains."

"Oh," I continued. "You wouldn't happen to have any of those lying around?" I smiled sweetly and sarcastically fluttered my eyelashes at him.

"I'll see what I can do," He answered nonchalantly.

Oh. I hadn't been serious about him having silver chains. I stopped again and looked up at him curiously, wondering if he was just messing with me. When he showed no signs of pointing at me and saying *gotcha*, I decided to push things a little further. "So it's true that silver affects werewolves?"

"Only the newly turned. Silver loses its potency after the first few shifts."

I nodded, feeling incredibly silly for quizzing a stranger about werewolves. "Now the question is, how do you know about all of this, and how can you expect me to believe it?"

Jason ignored my question and began walking again.

"Hey!" I shouted. "What gives? I was honest with you, wasn't I? I think I deserve an answer."

He stopped and turned to consider me, concern plain on his face. We had neared the city park. He jerked his head slightly, gesturing for me to follow him. We trod a short distance more through the grass, then stepped onto the slightly damp sand of the currently empty playground. Jason sat down on the black rubber seat of a chain-link swing and motioned for me to take the swing next to him.

"To answer one of your questions, I expect you to believe everything about Dan being a werewolf, because you already do. You wouldn't have walked out here with me if you hadn't already caught on. In answer to the question of how I know about these things, I will make you a deal," Jason smiled. "Let us handle this situation with Lucy, as we're running out of time, then I will tell you anything you wish to know."

"Anything?" I questioned.

"Anything."

I glared at him skeptically, but then conceded, I didn't really have much choice but to trust him, for Lucy's sake. We sat on the swings discussing Lucy's "problem". Well, mostly I sat scraping the toes of my shoes in the damp sand as my swing drifted back and forth while Jason tried to explain to me exactly what was going to happen to Lucy that night.

I was relieved to have someone that at least knew something of what was going on. I knew I should have a million questions for him, but besides the question of how he knew about werewolves, I was at a loss. I gripped the chains of the swing, squeezing hard enough to make oval indents in my palms, trying to remain steady. I just had to hold on until the night was through. After that I could fall apart.

Our conversation had ebbed, then Jason asked suddenly, "If you were so suspicious about Dan, why did you go out with him on Saturday?"

I gave him an 'isn't it obvious' look. "Lucy and Al were set on going. I couldn't let them go alone."

"But what good did you hope to accomplish by going with? How did you intend to protect them?"

I paused in consternation. How did I intend to protect them? Truthfully, I hadn't though about it. I just knew that I had to go with them. At least that way, I'd know that I had tried. I answered, frustrated with my inability to explain, "I just had to go, even if I couldn't do any good, I couldn't let them go alone."

"You're a good friend," he stated simply.

"Exactly." I smiled at him, happy with his ability to sum up my situation.

With that, he rose from his swing and I followed suit. We started walking back toward the school. I amused myself by watching my sneakers as they squashed down the blades of moist green grass. We'd run out of werewolf conversation, so we walked in silence. Surprisingly, the silence wasn't awkward.

I stumbled on a loose rock at one point and slipped backward on the grass. I had closed my eyes, waiting for my butt to hit the ground, when I realized that Jason had caught me with his hands under my upper arms, right before I hit. One moment he had been beside me, and the next he was in position to catch me, too fast for me to follow.

My heart fluttered. Please don't let him be another werewolf. He hoisted me back up and smiled at my mumbled thank you. I walked a little ahead of him after that, trying to hide my bright red embarrassed face as well as my cautious eyes.

We walked up to the school parking lot just as Lucy and Allison arrived. Jason nodded to Lucy and left, saying he would meet us at my house. I watched him walk to what was apparently his car. Now I don't know cars, but this one looked expensive . . . and fast. The paint was a glossy charcoal gray that would be mistaken for black in the night. Nice.

Allison broke me out of my daydream of getting into that car with Jason. "So *that's* where you were."

I gave her a quizzical look.

"During geometry. Not that I condone ditching, but he looks like a pretty good reason."

"That was Jason, the guy we met in the woods. I'll explain on the way to my house," I answered.

We piled into Allison's car for the short ride to my house. Lucy in front and me in the back for a change.

As soon as we pulled out of the parking lot, Lucy turned to look at me in the backseat. "I thought we didn't trust him," she said, referring to Jason.

I met her eyes. "I'm not sure that we do, but he admitted to knowing more about Dan than he let on. Dan is in fact a werewolf, or so I'm told, and Jason seems to know quite a bit about werewolves, so we need his help, trust or no trust."

Lucy looked down for a moment, then met my eyes steadily. "Did he say how likely it is that I'm . . . infected?"

I patted her shoulder, trying to be comforting and failing. I answered honestly, "He said it's a good possibility."

Lucy turned back around to stare out her window.

I went on, speaking to the back of Lucy's head, "Let's just try and not worry too much until we actually know what's going on. Jason and Dan could both just be crazy. We're only going along with any of this to err on the side of caution."

Lucy gave the barest of nods, but stayed staring out at the passing trees.

"So . . . same plan still?" Allison asked hesitantly.

"We're going to tweak it just a little," I replied, then went on to detail my conversation with Jason.

By the time we arrived at my house we had agreed on the rough plan. Jason would obtain restraints for

Lucy, we would restrain her, and then we would wait. So, not the most elaborate plan, but better than nothing.

We went inside and Lucy and I journeyed to the kitchen to scrounge for food, our stomachs growling for having missed lunch. My bright, sunny kitchen, with walls painted a yellow so light it's almost white seemed out of place with our current moods. Maple cabinets, white tile counter tops, and plenty of plants in multicolored ceramic pots complete the cozy, cottage-like feel. I could tell that Lucy felt anything but cozy.

We found my mom standing by the coffee pot, drinking a freshly made cup. My mom and I are different in a lot of ways, but we both run on the same fuel—coffee. We had actually recently agreed to try and cut back. It wasn't going too well.

All we could find to eat was a box of macaroni and cheese of indeterminate age and some rice cakes. Mac and cheese it was. I set about making it while my mom quizzed us about our day at school, receiving only vague and generic answers. Once the mac and cheese was done I divided it into blue ceramic bowls. I grabbed a cup of coffee, standing by my conviction that coffee goes with everything, and Lucy and I went into the dining room to sit and eat at the pale wood table.

I watched Lucy out of the corner of my eye as we ate. She rubbed her arm, with a nervous strain to her face. Allison had stayed in the kitchen to talk to my mom. I eavesdropped until Allison mentioned a sale at a local boutique, then quickly tuned them out. I focused on making myself swallow the macaroni. Yeah, I was beginning to get an idea of its age.

As we finished eating, my mom came into the dining room and grabbed our bowls to stack in the dishwasher. Lucy and I headed upstairs to my room. Allison said a quick goodbye to my mom, then followed us up. We sat on my plush beige carpeting pow-wow style.

"So tell me more about Jason," Allison began.

Rolling my eyes, I answered, "We don't know much, just what we told you about what happened in the woods."

Allison pouted at the lack of details on the new cute boy.

"So he knows about werewolves?" Lucy interjected.

"Um, apparently so," I replied. "I asked him how he knew, but he said he'd explain it later."

"I'm not sure how I feel about him being involved," Lucy said. "We know even less about him than we do about Dan. Why wouldn't he tell you how he knew about all of this werewolf stuff? For all we know he could be working with Dan."

I shrugged. I didn't want to tell her that I was simply acting on my gut instinct in trusting him. "What choice do we have?"

Lucy's face screwed up in consternation. "Good point."

"Plus," Allison added. "You must admit, the boy is not bad to look at." I rolled my eyes at her and she went on, "C'mon Xoe, don't act like you didn't notice, I saw you making moon-eyes at him as he went to his car, and don't get me started on the car." She smiled with a sigh and looked away, as if imaging the car in her mind.

"Okay," I conceded. "I admit that he is not bad to look at, but there are much more pressing issues to focus on."

Allison dismissed me with a wave of her hand. "When is he supposed to come?"

"I don't know . . . " I began to reply when I was interrupted by a knock on my bedroom door.

My mom waited for me to open the door, then gave me her best scrutinizing look.

"What?" I asked, confused.

She placed her hands on her hips. "Did you forget to tell me something?"

I gave her a blank stare.

She continued, "Care to explain why two young men are waiting downstairs?"

Two? "Oh, er, um, just friends coming over to study mom, geez," I replied as nonchalantly as possible.

She walked away with a look of motherly knowing and I followed her downstairs.

The second boy in question was Max, who stood just inside the closed front door. The very Max that had been sitting with Dan the dreadful day that

Allison dragged him to our lunch table. Max was short for a guy, about 5'4". He had shaggy, sandy blond hair and the kind of complexion that would freckle like crazy if Shelby ever got any measure of sun. His pale green eyes were staring intently at the floor while his hands nervously straightened his striped polo shirt and khaki cargo pants.

I raised an eyebrow at Jason, wanting an explanation for Max's presence. He was still dressed in his flannel and jeans. He glanced toward the ceiling and gave his head a slight nod, signaling that we should go upstairs. I was instantly suspicious of how he knew my bedroom was upstairs, but soon felt silly when I realized he had seen me come down as he waited at the door.

Sighing, I invited Max and Jason to my room where Lucy and Allison waited. They followed me upstairs without a word. We entered my room and I shut the door so that the questioning could begin.

The second the latch clicked, I whirled on Jason. "What is *he* doing here?" I spat, pointing my finger at Max. "He's in league with Dan, I *saw* them sitting together."

"Hey!" Max interrupted. "I'm not in *league* with him. I could tell he was a wolf, so I tried to talk to the guy, then I realized that he's completely nuts." He crossed his arms, looking like a grumpy elf.

Wait, a *wolf*? "Don't tell me you're one too," I groaned.

"Well yeah," Max answered, holding his head high, "but I'm not a bad one, I'm here to help." His head remained high, proud to not be a "bad one".

I turned back to Jason as he started pulling things out of a dark blue backpack to show to us: a length of shiny silver chain, two sets of handcuffs, and a medical case. Lucy looked ready to pass out.

"What's in the case?" I asked.

"Tranquilizers," Jason answered, shifting his focus from his "supplies" to acknowledge me. Taking in my shocked expression, he elaborated. "First we'll chain her up. The chains and cuffs are solid silver. Then if she starts to change, we tranquilize her. It won't stop the change, but it will slow it down and stop her from hurting herself." He opened the medical case and showed us several syringes and vials of clear liquid.

Lucy had now gone from pale to green. Allison noticed and sat Lucy down on my bed. Jason looked questioningly at Lucy, deep blue eyes pinched with concern.

I didn't feel too hot myself. I do *not* like needles. Even thinking about getting a shot makes me queasy, and getting blood drawn, forget about it. I can't even watch people get shots on TV. There is a very justified reason why my ears aren't pierced.

"Well it's only 5:00 right now," Allison announced, taking everyone's attention off the tranquilizers. "What time is she supposed to *change* at?"

"Full dark," Max responded. "Around 8:00. We shouldn't do it here though. Jason found a place."

We all looked at Jason still squatting on the floor beside his backpack. He stared back.

"Lead on," I said in a booming voice, dramatically thrusting my arm toward the door.

Jason chuckled. He was the only one. At least someone found me amusing.

Jason gathered the supplies and shoved them back into his backpack, then we all trooped out of my room and downstairs single file. I told my mom we were staying at Lucy's. Luckily I hadn't mentioned to my mom that Lucy's parents weren't in town. At her further questioning I answered that of course the boys were going home by nine, and out we went into the crisp evening air.

Jason's nifty car was waiting out front for us. Apparently my wish for a ride was about to be fulfilled, if not in the same fashion I had imagined. Jason opened the car door and lowered himself into the driver's seat, unlocking the other doors as he did so. I snagged the front passenger seat, leaving everyone else to pile into the back. Lucy ended up squished in the middle between Allison and Max. Jason started the ignition and the David Bowie CD that was in his player started to play. A man after my own heart. Away we went, into the unknown.

10

We drove away from town to the mostly abandoned industrial district, passing by empty lots and dilapidated buildings as we went. The slowly eroding buildings were all a depressing gray that caused them to blend in with the murky sky. The district has the feel of a ghost town. Only transients and other seedy characters dwell there these days.

I glanced at the door to make sure it was locked, then looked at Lucy's face in the rear view mirror. She had her eyes pinched shut like she was trying to pretend that nothing was happening. I couldn't imagine how she felt. I was scared enough just being involved in the situation. Lucy had to face the fact that she might become a werewolf in a world where we would have never imagined such things existed.

The crunch of gravel on asphalt along with the

slowing of the car brought my attention back to our surroundings. Jason had pulled into the back lot of an empty, cavernous warehouse and was driving into an already opened bay. Once inside, he parked, then we all got out to survey our surroundings. Jason walked back to shut the bay door behind us while Max took several electric camping lanterns out of the trunk of Jason's car.

Max turned on each lantern as he placed them around the expansive, creepy, dusty room. I looked up and everything was black, there was no telling how high the ceiling was. I felt the darkness pressing down on me, inciting panic, like reverse claustrophobia. I took slow breaths, in and out, hoping no one noticed. I drew my hand over the beads of cold sweat that had formed on my brow.

As Max's lanterns filled the warehouse with a dull glow, I took more of a look around. Trash and what appeared to be old clothes littered the floor, giving off an unpleasant, mildewy smell. The area where Max was setting up the lanterns had been swept clean of debris. I tried to distract myself by attempting to make out some of the graffiti that covered the walls until Max walked back toward us.

"You ready?" Max asked Lucy, who was huddling next to me looking terrified.

"B-but, it's only 6:00," Lucy stammered.

Max shrugged. "Better safe than sorry."

I put my arm around Lucy's shoulders, acting

calmer than I felt, and walked her to a metal-framed folding chair that Max had placed in the center of the lanterns. Jason approached with the chains and cuffs.

Jason faced Lucy. "Go ahead and sit down," he told her.

Lucy slowly sat on the black canvas seat of the rickety metal chair, then looked up at Jason with huge, terrified eyes. "What next?"

"Hold out your hands." Jason set the chains and cuffs on the cement floor and demonstrated by holding his hands in front of him, wrists side by side. Lucy slowly complied, but was trembling so badly that she could barely hold her wrists together.

Jason picked up one set of cuffs and knelt by Lucy. He gingerly cuffed her hands together, running the cuff on her right hand through a link of the chain before locking the cuff down. He then put the second pair of cuffs around her ankles and attached the other end of the chain, kind of hog-tying her. Then, using a big padlock, he attached the loose ends of chain to a metal loop coming out of the concrete ground. I hadn't noticed the loop before, and wondered what its original purpose was. Finished, Jason backed away to survey his handiwork.

"Is that it?" I asked. "It doesn't seem very . . . restraining."

Jason turned his attention to me. "It will be when she's in wolf form. She'll be a lot bigger than she is now. We don't want the chains to hurt her when she changes."

Oh, well that made sense . . . I guess.

Lucy watched us with big, terrified eyes. I went and sat on the bare concrete beside her, taking her hand in mine. The cold from the ground seeped into my body. Everybody else sat in a semicircle in front of us.

"How did you know Dan was crazy?" I asked, turning to Max.

He gave me a confused look.

I elaborated, "In my room, you said you tried to get to know Dan and you realized he was crazy. How'd you know?"

Max hesitated. "Um, you know, just by the kind of things he talked about . . . "

I fixed him with a stubborn stare, crossed my arms, and raised my eyebrows, urging him on.

"He told me to stay away from Lucy, because she was his. He told me I could have Allison if I wanted." Max paused at an 'as if' noise from Allison.

"What about me?" I interjected.

That confused look crossed Max's face again.

"What?" I asked snarkily. "You said that Dan claimed Lucy and you could have Allison, what am I, chopped liver?"

Jason chimed in with a smirk on his face, "You're mad that no one claimed you as property?"

I gave him a petulant look. "It's the principle of the thing." I turned back toward Max. "Well?"

"He didn't include you because you can't be turned," Max replied.

Now it was my turn for the confused expression.

Max went on, "Only humans can be turned."

Jason gave Max a sharp look. I looked back and forth between Max and Jason, trying to understand the warning look on Jason's face and the confused one on Max's.

"She doesn't know," Jason said softly.

"Oh," Max murmured. "Sorry."

"Ok, someone needs to tell me what's going on here," I interrupted.

"I don't think you want to know," Jason said softly.

"Try me."

Jason turned to me, looking resigned, he explained, "Supernatural beings are usually equipped with a way to tell their own. To a werewolf, humans have a certain smell, and anything not human will smell different. They may not be able to decipher what type of being you are, but they can tell if you aren't human. You don't smell human."

I gave him a smug look, despite my sudden loss of breath. I managed to suck in enough air to reply, "Of course I'm human, my mom's human, and as far as I know I've never been bitten by any sort of supernatural beastie."

"You never knew your dad," Allison countered, catching on to what was being implied. "Your mom's human, but you have no idea what your dad could've been."

"For someone who was still skeptical about the werewolf thing, you seem all too ready to believe that my dad was some sort of . . . non-human," I shot back.

Allison frowned. "Just think about it, Xoe."

The superior look faded from my face. "But . . . I'm sure my mom would have known if my dad had been less than human, and if she knew, she would have told me." It sounded a weak defense, even to me.

"Would you have ever guessed that Max wasn't human?" Allison asked quietly.

A stab of fear entered my heart. "No, but I don't really know Max. My mom *knew* my dad. He *had* to have been human," I said in a last ditch effort to prove them wrong.

Jason wouldn't meet my eyes. "I am sorry Xoe, but . . . your smell begs to differ."

"Well, then . . . what am I?" I asked no one in particular.

Max shrugged. "Not sure, it's not a smell I know."

We all sat in silence. If my mind wasn't already spinning, it sure was now. I had just begun to accept the idea that supernatural beings existed. Now I was supposed to believe that I was one?

"So that's it?" I asked, frustrated. "You tell me that I'm not human and have no explanation other than that I smell funny?"

Jason shifted to sit in a more comfortable position.

"Has anything strange ever happened to you, or have you ever been able to do something you should not have been able to do?"

"Not that I know of," I answered hesitantly.

"Then there is no way to tell," Jason stated. "You may simply go on like a regular human."

"Is there any reason why I wouldn't?" I asked. "I mean, if I was going to exhibit any non-human traits, wouldn't I have done so by now?"

"Not necessarily," Jason answered. "Mixing human bloodlines with supernatural is a *roll-of-the-dice* process. There is no way of telling what might happen. Humans have dominant and recessive traits. The supernatural traits are no different from the others. They may be recessive to the human ones . . . or the supernatural traits may only reveal themselves with time."

"Oh," I answered. What else could I say?

"What time is it now?" Lucy asked the room anxiously. I wanted Jason to continue his explanation, but I couldn't blame Lucy for changing the subject. I'd just have to ask him later.

Max glanced at his watch. "6:25."

Lucy cringed. "When did you say it was going to happen again . . . the *change*?"

Max watched Lucy worriedly. "Around full dark, it's not exactly precise. We'll just have to wait and see."

Lucy was silent for a moment, then asked hesitantly, "Will it hurt?"

Max smiled sadly. "Do you want the truth?"

Lucy seemed to think about it, then nodded her head slowly, as if she might regret learning the answer.

"Yes," Max replied, "it hurts."

Lucy nodded her head somberly. I squeezed her hand, and we settled in to wait.

Only a few minutes had gone by when a horrible thought dawned on me, and my mouth went dry with fear. I turned toward Max. "Um, aren't *you* supposed to be turning into a werewolf tonight too?"

Max smiled. "I can control it. I have to turn each month, but I can do it any of the three days that the moon is at its fullest."

Allison looked green. "Are you sure?" she asked.

Max nodded, perfectly at ease. We had no choice but to take him for his word and hope that it held true. Well, that, or kick him out the bay door, but that would be just plain rude.

The next hour went by incredibly slow. My mind was completely preoccupied with the idea that I might not be human. Conversation was kept to a minimum, not by choice, but what do you say when you just found out you might not be human, all while waiting for your friend to turn into a wolf? It was almost 8:00. There was no light left outside to shine through the bottom of the bay door where it met the ground.

Suddenly Lucy started to whimper. "Something's happening," she spat through gritted teeth.

I let go of Lucy's hand and stood. Jason ran to his

medical kit and started filling a syringe. Lucy's knuckles were white as her hands curled into tight fists. Sweat began to bead on her brow. Jason came running with the syringe and unceremoniously stuck her in the arm.

Lucy panted heavily, her eyes half closed. Then the screaming started.

Jason came up behind Lucy and quickly tied a thick piece of cloth around her mouth to dull the noise of her screams. It didn't help much. We just had to hope that no one was in hearing range of us. Loud popping noises emanated from her limbs and there was a sickening tearing sound coming from somewhere in her body. Her skin began to ripple like something alive swam underneath. Her bones pulled apart at the joints under her skin. Her body twisted and reshaped as her form started to look more wolf than human.

Harsh reality set in. It was real. It was all real. Werewolves and who knew what else . . . existed. I was frozen with terror as I watched Lucy change. Fur erupted all over her mostly wolf body. It was like freeze frame animation, every time I blinked, the picture changed.

A few heart-pounding minutes later, Lucy's screams were cut off into a guttural howl. My limbs unlocked and I ran to a corner and threw up. Hot tears stung my eyes as I crouched in the corner, not wanting to look back to the thing that was formerly Lucy.

When I had regained enough composure to turn back to the scene, a giant wolf had taken Lucy's place. It was growling and thrashing around, trying to free itself from its bonds. The warped chair was lying several feet away from the wolf. Large gleaming teeth snapped at empty air as the wolf strained against the chains. The gag had fallen to the floor. The wolf's fur was the same black as Lucy's hair.

11

The wolf continued to thrash and snap at the air. Jason herded us away, back toward his car. "She'll be like this the rest of the night. I'll stay with her. Max can take you guys home," Jason stated, annoyingly calm.

"Will she be like this every month?" Allison asked breathlessly. Her eyes were too wide and I half expected her to bolt out of the building at any second.

"No," Max answered, his hand on Allison's arm, offering comfort. "She'll slowly gain control of herself in wolf form. Once she's a little less dangerous, I'll take her to shift in the woods. Eventually she'll be able to go out on her own and not risk eating any humans."

"How long?" I asked.

"I don't really know," Max replied. "The only experience I have to go on is my own. It took me about five months, five shifts. Those first few months . . . I don't really remember much of what happened . . . "

Max's far-away gaze made him look like a lost little boy. I realized that I knew barely anything about Max. I had always just kind of . . . overlooked him. He had gone through everything that Lucy had, but he had been completely by himself. Until now, he had lived in a world where no one was like him—alone. I felt a wash of love and gratitude for my friends. With them I would never feel that lonely. I needed to stop taking that for granted.

I shifted my attention to Allison as she nodded, numbly accepting Max's answer, then slid into the backseat of Jason's car.

"I'm staying," I stated matter-of-factly. "My mom thinks I'm at Lucy's and I'm not leaving her. She'll be scared when she turns back."

Jason looked unsure, but finally nodded his assent. Allison stayed staring blankly in the backseat, looking pale. I put Allison's seatbelt on her without her really noticing, then grabbed a piece of gum from her purse while I was at it to get rid of the taste of vomit in my mouth. I gave Allison one final worried look, then shut the car door.

After Max and Allison drove away, Jason and I sat cross-legged on the floor, a safe distance from Lucy. Jason had taken a brown leather aviator jacket out of his car before Max drove away. I had assumed it was for him, but as we sat down he draped it over my shoulders. I was freezing, so I didn't argue. I put my arms through the sleeves and wrapped the jacket close around me. His jacket smelled like him, the scent smelled like a pleasant mixture of trees and vanilla. The cold didn't seem to faze him.

I was the first to break the silence. "Tell me more about werewolves."

He looked up at me, his face half in shadow. "Max would really be the one to ask. I have already told you most of what I know: they must turn once a month, but once they gain control they are able to change at will; they have superhuman strength, even in human form; they are not much stronger than humans in the beginning, but the strength grows as time goes on; and they are very hard to kill, depending on how powerful they are. Like I said, silver only works on newer werewolves."

The strength thing was new information to me. I cocked my head, thinking. "So how do you kill an experienced werewolf?"

"It is no easy task," he replied. "Brute force is the best method. The older the wolf, the more quickly it will regenerate. You literally have to tear them limb from limb."

I suddenly felt queasy again. "So a human wouldn't be able to kill one?"

Jason shook his head. "It has been done before, though it's usually a group of humans. One human would stand no chance, unless they were very lucky."

I nodded, my fear of Dan now increased ten-fold. I still had one more question that had been eating at me all day. Okay, more like three. "How did you just happen to show up in town shortly after Dan did, and how did you know to be on the trail when he attacked me and Lucy, and how do you know about were-wolves?" I kept my eyes focused steadily on Jason, trying to keep myself distracted from the all too real wolf salivating across the room.

Jason ran his hand through his hair, then returned it to his knee. I was beginning to understand that it was his nervous gesture, the 'tell' that gave him away. He took in a deep breath. "I've been following Dan."

"Why?" I prodded. I realized that I had scooted a little too near Jason in anticipation of his answer. His face was very close. I felt a blush heat my face, but held my ground.

Jason either was comfortable with the closeness, or else he didn't notice. "Most werewolves are able to fit into society. They form packs for protection and do their best to play human. Dan was a member of a pack, but then he attacked and killed a human. Pack law states that if any wolf kills a human, that wolf will be executed. Dan fled. His pack hired me to follow him. Once he entered an area with a local pack, I was to report to them and they would handle the execution. Dan has been very careful so far. Shelby does not have a local pack, so I was keeping an eye on him until he moved on."

I thought about what he'd said for a moment. "Why can't you just, you know, *take care of it*?"

He laughed and drew a little closer to me. "Trust me, I have considered it. First of all, it would be a close fight, Dan is very strong. Secondly, the wolves tend to keep these things within their society. I was only hired to follow him."

I asked, "So you're like a bounty hunter?"

The side of his mouth raised in a crooked smile. "Something like that."

Hmm, a real live bounty hunter. I tried to hide my morbid excitement. "So, if werewolves stay in packs, then why is Max in Shelby, where there is no pack?"

Jason answered, "I have not asked him his story. He apparently changed on his own, so I would guess that he was attacked by a rogue wolf. It is rare for someone like that to not only survive the attack and the change, but to also not massacre his loved ones, but it happens.Any more questions?"

"Yes," I replied. "Who . . . or what, are you, and how did you become involved in all of this?"

He pursed his lips. "That I will explain when this night is over, and you are not trapped alone in a dark room with me and a bloodthirsty wolf."

Ominous . . . very ominous. "Tomorrow?"

He sighed, then looked down and nodded his head. "Tomorrow."

Jason looked over at Lucy and my eyes followed his. She had calmed down, and had now resorted to staring at us hungrily. It was hard to think of the wolf as my best friend. Usually best friends didn't want to eat you. She kept her eyes on us, ears forward and alert.

"Max is back," Jason stated.

The bay door lifted and Max called in that it was him, confirming what Jason had said, then drove Jason's car through, casting bouncing shapes across the rubble against the walls of the warehouse with the headlights.

"Is Allison okay?" I called as Max stepped out of the car.

"She's adjusting, I think. It's a lot to take in." Max said as he went to close the bay door. After an echoing clang, Max walked to where we were sitting and plunked down beside Jason. He turned to me. "There're some blankets in the back seat if you want to get some rest, Xoe."

Come to think of it, I was *exhausted*. Max looked as annoyingly wide-awake as ever. I nodded and got up.

Crawling into the backseat of the car, I found several blankets and a pillow waiting for me. Bonus points for Max, or Jason, depending on who had supplied me with the bedding.I considered giving Jason back his jacket, which was still wrapped around me, but greedily snuggled up with it.I awkwardly curled my legs up on the seat. Believe it or not, there are some downsides to being tall. I fell asleep about 30 seconds after my head hit the pillow.

I had nightmares of werewolves, vampires, and my dad, who I somehow just knew was my dad, even though I've never seen him, turning into a gargantuan monster and telling me I'd grow up to be just like him.

I woke to Jason gently shaking my shoulders. "Lucy's starting to change back," he informed me. He looked at me worriedly and placed his hand against my neck. "You have a fever."

I blinked at him, momentarily confused, and mumbled, "I'm fine, it's nothing. I need to see Lucy."

I scooted out of the car in a hurry, but was instantly stopped by Max. He grabbed my arm to keep me from rushing to Lucy and pulled one of the blankets out of the car. He blushed, handing me the dark gray blanket, and said "She's not going to, um, have any clothes when she changes back."

"Oh," I replied, clutching the blanket in both hands, "er, thanks."

I gathered up the blanket so it wouldn't drag on the floor and started walking to Lucy. I spared a glance back to Jason and Max, who were standing dutifully by the car with their backs turned to Lucy and me. I wished I could wait with them. I wondered if Lucy was going to be different, more like Dan. I hoped not.

Lucy was almost back to human form by the time I reached her. She was lying on her side on the concrete, still in chains. Her body was back to normal, but her face was still . . . wrong. It was hard to tell what was wrong about it, it just was. She was panting and whimpering softly. I watched her worriedly, feeling sick again.

I couldn't make sense of the change, but her face slowly shifted back to normal. I wrapped the blanket around her, snuggling it up around her neck. Tears streamed down her delicate face as I called Jason over to unlock her chains. After letting the chains fall to the floor, Jason gently lifted Lucy in his arms. She was mostly covered by the blanket, only her bare feet and a few locks of her long black hair were visible. He carried her to the car, placing her in the back seat.

I followed them and slid into the backseat beside Lucy, comforting her while Jason and Max loaded everything back into the trunk. She laid her head in my lap and I stroked her hair while she cried silent, tired tears. With a slam of the trunk, Jason and Max walked to the front of the car. I looked down at Lucy and realized that she'd fallen asleep in my lap.

Jason slid into the driver's seat as Max took the front seat next to him. Neither looked back at Lucy and me. Jason started the car, lighting up the clock on the dash. I spared a glance at it, 6:27 am. We were *so* not making school today. I put my seatbelt on and awkwardly wrapped the middle seatbelt around Lucy's waist, snapping it in place.

I directed Jason as he drove us to Lucy's empty house. The warmth of the sun from the window pulsed against my skin. I propped Lucy up so I could take off Jason's jacket. Lucy was still unconscious, her limbs limp like those of a corpse. Jason pulled into the circular gravel driveway and shut off the car. He got out and opened the door to the backseat while Max took Lucy's keys to unlock the front door. Jason gently lifted Lucy out of the car and carried her inside with me tagging along behind him.

I flipped on the lights as I walked through the doorway, then led everyone into the living room so that Jason could place the still unconscious Lucy gently on the pale beige couch. Everything about Lucy's house is very . . . beige. It was a stark contrast to the colorful chaos that I was used to.

We stood in the silence of the dark, nondescript living room until Max said, "She'll be out for a while, TV?"

I grabbed the remote from the plain oak coffee table, turning the TV on as I sat down next to Max on the love seat. Jason had sat down by Lucy's feet on the couch. I flipped through the channels, finally settling on *Teen Wolf* the movie. Seemed fitting.

As we watched, I quizzed Max on the similarities between the movie and real werewolves. He seemed more than happy to talk about it. He chattered away while I half-listened to him. Jason appeared to be deep in thought, not watching the movie or listening to Max. I settled back on the love seat and prepared to wait. Eventually Max ran out of material. After all, everything he knew about werewolves was what he had learned from personal experience, and I turned my focus back to the movie.

When the movie ended, I pushed the *guide* button on the remote. Apparently there exists a second *Teen Wolf* movie, titled *Teen Wolf Too*, which was playing after the first one. Lucy was still out cold, so we decided to watch that one too. Eventually I curled up against the arm of the love seat and let my eyes drift closed. My sleep was never restful when I had my fever-inducing dreams, so I still felt exhausted.

I woke up to Max reaching across me to retrieve the remote. The credits were rolling on *Teen Wolf Too,* and Max quickly changed the channel to a soccer game. I looked at Jason to find him watching me, worry creasing his brow. Jason caught my eyes with his, then nodded to the backdoor. Interpreting his signal, I followed him out, leaving Max to watch Lucy.

"I guess I can tell you what you want to know now," Jason said with a sigh as I shut the backdoor behind us. "Dan is still in town, so the situation is far from over, but at least now you have a choice of whether or not you want to be around me." He walked further through the grass to sit on a small iron bench near the white fence that surrounded Lucy's backyard. A large oak tree shaded the bench, its branches reaching hungrily toward the sun. He gestured for me to sit beside him. Sitting down, I watched him expectantly.

"I'm what popular culture would view as a vampire," he said.

I blinked slowly at him. "Come again?"

Instead of repeating himself, he looked down at his lap while I processed his answer.

"Well I guess that makes sense." I said after a few moments of silence.

He looked up as a stunned expression crossed his face. "You're not shocked? Horrified?"

I smirked. "You're talking to someone who found out that werewolves exist, had her best friend turned into a werewolf, not to mention finding out that I'm apparently not human, all in the last few days. Forgive me if I do not display the proper amount of awe. As for the horrified part, that all depends on my next few questions." On the inside I was shaking, but it wasn't time to break down. Not yet.

He looked at me, slightly confused, as if he could see right through to my soul. It was all too reminiscent of Dan's looks during English. "Go on," he prompted me, anxiety creeping into his normally controlled voice.

"Do you drink blood?" I asked.

He nodded. "I only drink animal blood now, or human blood from blood banks when I can manage it."

I hesitated on the *now*. "But you at one time drank directly from humans?"

He nodded again.

I continued. "So . . . you've killed people?"

He looked at the ground, then answered me while

focusing on the grass at our feet. "That was a long time ago. My bloodlust used to be much more difficult to control. I felt remorse for those I killed, but I could not stop."

My pulse sped, and I had to resist the overwhelming urge to scoot away from him. "So what changed?" I asked softly.

Jason answered, very carefully avoiding my eyes, "One night, a child became my prey. He was alone, walking to his home at night. He must have only been seven or eight years old. I followed him, at war with myself . . . a war I always lost. It became too much, I approached him and knocked him to the ground. I was poised to go for his throat. Then I saw the look on his face. He seemed so shocked that someone would hurt him. He looked at me, not understanding what I intended, and I was somehow able to stop. That had never happened before. Until then, once I had spotted my prey, I would try to resist, but then my conscience would turn off, my mind would become entirely consumed by the hunt. After that night, I was able to stop it, I do not know why. Once I had a choice, I began to feed only on animals or on blood from humans after they had donated it." He paused, staring at the ground. "Does that change things for you?" At my puzzled look he added, "Does it cause you think less of me?"

Ooh, tricky. I thought for a moment, staring off into space while trying to ignore the sick feeling in my gut, then turned to find him staring at me intently, blue eyes unblinking. "I don't know," I answered. "I'll need some time to think about it."

He looked back down and nodded, resigned.

"Okay, next question, how are you out in the sun?" I asked.

He laughed a slightly bitter laugh. "It is a myth that we burn in the sun. The sun hurts my eyes, and my vision is slightly less during the day. I suppose it is because of my increased night-vision."

I nodded. "How old are you?" I asked.

"I was born in 1883," He smiled. "Anything else?"

I gulped. That made him . . . old. I took a deep breath and let it out. "I thought you talked kind of funny."

He smiled and tentatively took my hand. He was being honest with me, so I let him. He gripped a little harder. "Your hand is trembling."

Damn, and here I though I was acting all cool and collected. "So maybe I am a *little* shocked by the vampire thing," I mumbled.

He said nothing, but kept his hand in mine.

I was reminded of a question I had meant to ask him last night. "Where are you staying while you're here?"

"I'm currently residing at the *Holiday Inn* in town."

I laughed. I couldn't help it.

"What?" he asked.

"The *Holiday Inn*, it just seems so . . . normal."

"Would you rather I was staying at the local crypt

perhaps? Or possibly you know of a cozy bat infested cave nearby?"

Grinning, I answered, "At the very least you could have chosen a creepy abandoned building or something."

"I may be a *creature of the night*," he wiggled the fingers of his free hand in the air in mock spookiness, "but I happen to enjoy running water and electricity."

I snapped my fingers in an *aw shucks* gesture and said mournfully, "You've shattered all of my illusions."

Jason laughed, but quickly took on a more somber tone. "I can track Dan on my own, leave you alone, but it would be safer if I stayed with you and Lucy."

I took me a moment to realize that he expected an answer."Oh, stay, of course you should stay with us."

I sensed relief in his smile. I wasn't sure why that surprised me.

"Lucy's up!" a call came from the house.

I leapt up and went running inside with Jason following shortly behind me. Lucy was sitting up on the couch with her blanket wrapped tightly around her.

"How are you feeling?" I asked her.

She looked up to me. "Ok, I guess. My throat is killing me, from the screaming Max tells me. Other than that, I'm just tired."

I sat beside her and put my arm around her shoulders. "Do you remember anything?" I asked.

"Not really," she replied. "I remember arriving at

the warehouse, then I remember this morning, changing back. I didn't hurt anyone, did I? Where's Al?" She looked from me to Max.

"No, you didn't hurt anyone," I assured her. "Max took Allison home after you changed. She was a little shaken up." I didn't feel the need to mention that I had been rather shaken myself.

Lucy looked down at her lap. "So, what now?"

"We still have Dan to worry about," Jason answered. "He's going to come for you at some point, and we need to be ready when he does."

Jason carefully avoided my eyes. Lucy looked back and forth between us, picking up on the awkwardness. Our banter seemed to have only temporarily softened the fact that I was unsure if I could deal with his past.

"My parents are coming home tonight. They won't let us all stay here." Lucy stated. She looked up at me expectantly.

"My mom will let you stay at my place, but we'll have to sneak the boys in. Has anyone talked to Al yet?" I asked.

Everyone shook their heads.

"We'll call her from my house. I need to get there and delete the message I'm sure the school has left because of my absence before my mom gets home."

Lucy's eyes widened and Max added, "They already called here, message successfully erased."

Lucy let out a relieved breath. "Thanks." She wrapped the blanket tightly around herself, then went upstairs to pack her stuff, walking a little unsteadily. As she left she said, "I'll tell my parents we have to stay up late to finish a school project, so I need to stay at your place. It'll work at least for tonight . . . I hope."

"Fingers crossed," I said.

Lucy paused on the stairs with a sour expression on her face. "Do you guys mind waiting while I take a quick shower?"

"No, I was going to recommend that," I answered with a smile.

"Gee Xoe, you have such a way with words," Lucy said as she turned to continue up the stairs.

While we waited for Lucy to shower, I worried over Lucy's new *affliction.* I also worried about the vampire sitting next to me on the sofa and the werewolf lounging on the love seat. Not to mention that tonight I had to sneak said vampire and werewolf into my house while we waited to be attacked by another werewolf.

Since when was being a teenager so complicated?

Don't answer that.

12

As soon as we arrived at my house, I got out of the car and unlocked the front door. Jason and Max went in first to make sure nothing was amiss around the house. I checked the messages and erased the one from the school. The other message was from Allison, saying to call her as soon as I got home. I picked up the phone and dialed her number.

Allison answered after the first ring. "What took you so long!" she exclaimed. "I have been waiting here for hours for you to tell me what's going on!"

I laughed. "Calm down Al. Everyone's okay. We're back at my house now."

"I'll see you in ten," she said, then hung up.

I placed the phone back in its cradle just as Max and Jason returned to the living room. Lucy was curled up on the couch, staring at nothing.

"I'm in desperate need of a shower," I announced to the room. I looked toward Max and Jason, "You guys are free to use the guest bathroom if you want. There should be plenty of hot water."

Max shrugged, "I don't have any extra clothes. I'll probably just run home and shower." He turned to Jason. "Mind if I use your car?"

"It is all yours," Jason answered. "I have clothes in the trunk that I need to grab, then you can take it."

"It's settled then," I concluded. I informed Jason where the guest bathroom was, then ran upstairs and hopped in the shower.

Finally alone, I took a moment to process the events of the previous night and that morning. It was a lot to take in: werewolves, vampires, and whatever I was. That last part was by far the most troubling to me, not that the others were unimportant, far from it. My world was completely and utterly upside-down.

I thought about Jason being a vampire. I wasn't even really sure about what a vampire was. I mean, I had the movies and legends to go on, but how many of them were actually based on reality? All I knew for sure was that he drank blood, and despite popular belief, could go out in the sun.

Vampires, as a general consensus, were reanimated corpses. Jason had said when he was born, but not when or if he died. Maybe you were just born a vampire, not changed into one.

Then there was Jason's profession. Bounty hunter?

I guess that was actually my choice of words, but still. His contract against Dan seemed valiant enough, but what if his other jobs weren't quite as innocent? I wished I had thought of all of these questions earlier.

I finished showering and dried off. Then I went rummaging through my closet and pulled on a clean pair of jeans. I considered a turtleneck and vetoed the idea; I wasn't sure if Jason would think it was because of him and be offended. I decided on a plain black, v-neck short-sleeved shirt then headed back to the group. As I neared the end of the stairs, Jason turned his head to watch me for the rest of my descent.

His observant blue eyes had a hint of some emotion that I didn't understand, except that it made my heart hurt in a funny way. It seemed an admiring gaze, but there was some sadness underneath. He was freshly showered and wearing a blue cotton t-shirt that matched his eyes on top of jeans and his usual hiking boots.

Walking into the room I saw that Lucy was pretending to watch the soccer game with Max, who had apparently already gone home and showered, since he was now wearing a yellow button up shirt, rolled up at the sleeves, and some more khaki cargo pants. I knew I had taken a long time in the shower, but I hadn't realized just *how* long. Noticing my presence, Max and Lucy both turned to add their gazes to Jason's.

I cut the silence by asking, "Anyone hungry?"

The atmosphere eased as everyone admitted that they were starved. We all trooped to the kitchen. I searched my usually empty pantry as everyone else went to sit in the adjoining dining room. Like I said, we're big on take-out in my house, so I was surprised to find we had all of the ingredients for pancakes. Mom must have gone shopping. I had retrieved a big blue ceramic mixing bowl and had begun mixing the batter when the doorbell rang.

"That'll be Allison," I called. "I'll get it." I went into the living room and opened the door. I was surprised to find not Allison, but Brian waiting outside. He was dressed in a red t-shirt and jeans, topped by his Letterman's jacket.

"So you *are* alive!" he exclaimed. I stared blankly at him and he went on, "Well what was I supposed to think? There was that scene in English yesterday with that weirdo Dan. And you, him, and the other new guy that sat behind you obviously had some tension going on, then today none of you are there, and I didn't see Allison in gym either."

Jason chose that moment to walk up and stand behind me, almost touching. I could feel the line of his chest a hair's-breadth away from my back. The look Brian gave him was not a friendly one. Ignoring Brian's glare, Jason stepped closer. Now he actually was pressed against my back. I shivered, sensing the tension in Jason's body.

Brian tried to stare down Jason, but then seemed to think better of it, and gave his usual grin, if not an entirely happy one. He turned his gaze back to me. "Do I smell pancakes?" he asked mischievously. He didn't wait for an answer. I stood there dumbly as he pushed his way through the door with a very deliberate look at Jason. As Brian walked past us, I turned to Jason for help, but was only rewarded with a sarcastic 'nice going' look. He'd been trying to intimidate Brian into leaving, and I'd totally blown it.

I crossed my arms with an angry pout, then headed back into the kitchen. Jason shut and locked the door, then followed me.

Max had started cooking the pancakes while I was gone on my rarely used electric griddle. I made a mental note to start using it more. It really was a genius invention. No stove required and clean up consisted of wiping it down with a paper towel. Max had placed the first of the pancakes onto a platter he had to have found shoved in the back of one of our barren cupboards. Leaving Max to his work, I peeked into the dining room to see Lucy and Brian sitting at opposite ends of my pale wood table.

Shaking my head, I started the coffee while Jason hovered over me. I ground the beans, fresh ground is the only way to go, and put them in the paper filter. Jason remained standing in the kitchen, watching me as I grabbed some paper plates, coffee mugs, and juice for the non-coffee drinkers. So it was well past lunchtime, I simply could not have pancakes without coffee.

Jason darted occasional glances at the table where Brian was sitting, while he continued to hover over me almost possessively. If I didn't know any better, I'd say Jason was jealous. Well, considering I'd only known him a few days, I really didn't know any better. Not knowing whether to be flattered, or annoyed, I settled on a little bit of both, and tried to ignore Jason as much as possible.

I finished setting the table as Max set the heaping platter of pancakes in the center. I brought out the coffee pot and sat down. Jason and I were the only ones to fill our cups. Point for the vampire. I added cream, no sugar. Jason took his black.

Another knock on the door signaled Allison's arrival. Max got up to let her in. The rest of us sat eating our pancakes, Jason and I on one side of the table, Brian on the other, and Lucy at the head of the table. Allison waltzed in ahead of Max, wearing a lavender tunic-style tank top over skinny jeans and black ballet flats. She tossed her black and silver overnight bag on the floor in a corner of the dining room, then sat down next to Brian as Max sat on the other side of Jason.

Jason heaped more pancakes onto his plate. I didn't think vampires could eat people food, or drink coffee for that matter. Another myth I guess, I'd have to ask later. He drizzled maple syrup over his pile of pancakes and dug in. Allison gave me a questioning look at the sight of Brian and I mouthed, "Later."

"So, this is quite a gathering," Brian observed innocently, albeit a little sarcastically. "What have you all got planned this evening?"

We each darted nervous glances at our co-conspirators.

"School project," Lucy answered.

Brian smiled. "School project? What class do you all have together?"

In an attempt to save our ruse Allison answered, "They're helping me with a project for the yearbook committee."

Brian's look remained suspicious, but the questioning ended . . . for now.

Allison took the opportunity to change the subject. "Who made the pancakes?"

Max raised his hand with a grin.

Allison laughed and ran her hand through her loose, blonde hair. "Surprise, surprise, Xoe passes the cooking off on someone else."

"Hey!" I shouted playfully. "I mixed. That's cooking."

Allison jested, "Oooooh, she uses a spoon."

I pouted, glaring at Al, as everyone laughed. I wasn't actually upset. My cooking skills were often mocked. Plus, I kind of had it coming. I gave Al a hard time about one thing or another most every day.

After we finished eating, I hustled Brian out of the house, saying we had to get started on our "project." I walked him to the door, but before walking out he turned to me. "I don't trust Jason. If you need anything, call."

Ah, the testosterone was suffocating. I said goodbye and shut the door to find Jason watching me from across the room.

He walked up to me, hands in his pockets, acting perfectly at ease. "Boyfriend?" he questioned.

"No, not that it's any of your business," I sniffed, then walked to the dining room where everyone else was still sitting. I sat down as Jason came into the room, a small, satisfied smile on his face.

Jason took the chair beside me and put his arm across my chair back casually, then started detailing the battle plan for that night. I leaned forward slightly so that I wouldn't be touching Jason's arm. What was with all of the hovering? I decided to write it off as Jason just being a touchy-feely kind of person. So why did my heart speed every time such touching occurred?

Jason caught my gaze with his midnight blue eyes. "If Dan shows up, Xoe, you, Lucy, and Allison need to get to Allison's car, lock yourselves inside and start driving. Don't stop until I call you on Allison's cell to let you know it's safe to come back."

I felt an instant flush of anger at the fact that he wanted us to run. I managed to keep my cool, and leaned my back against his arm. Rather than voicing that I refused to run, I pointed out the other flaw in the plan. "What about my mom?"

Jason grimaced. "Sorry Xoe, forgot about that." He paused to think for a moment. "Okay, you can tell your mom that Dan is a burglar, then you can all get out of the house together. We just can't let your mom call the cops."

I nodded. "That will probably work. My mom is *so* not good in emergency situations, so she'll likely do whatever we tell her." I blew out a sigh. We'd have to worry about her inevitable questions later. Okay, so it was a flawed plan . . . better than nothing.

Jason smiled and removed his arm from my chair. "It's settled then."

I'm sure that Jason meant that we should still run, but all he had said was to "get out of the house." Now that, I could do. I nodded my final assent to the plan.

Shortly after we had settled what we would do, my mom came home, dressed in a navy business suit and heels; must have been an office day. Taking in the group of us, she looked at me with a smile and hands on her hips, waiting for an explanation.

"School project," I told her.

"Pizza!" she exclaimed, disappearing into the living room to order.

Max looked at me, bewildered. "Your mom is *so* cool."

I smiled. "Yeah, I'd say she's a keeper."

We all headed up to my room, telling my mom we were going to work on our project. Al and Max sat side by side on my bed, while the rest of us settled into a semi-circle on my plush beige carpeting.

Now that we had nothing to do but wait, we got a conversation going about school, of all things. While we talked, Jason got up and walked around my room, looking at pictures and any trinkets I had on my dresser.

I watched him as he picked up a picture my mom had taken of me on a camping trip. I was nine, and even more gangly looking than I am now. I was posing with a marshmallow on a stick, my mouth way more open than it needed to be. He smiled, not noticing my gaze. I quickly turned my attention back to the conversation, but of course, my mind wandered. I couldn't imagine Jason as a savage killer, but he was, at least at one time. I wasn't sure how much that bothered me.

After a while my mom knocked on the door. Not waiting for an answer, she came in carrying several pizza boxes. She handed me a stack of paper plates to pass out as Max and Al came to join us on the floor. My mom set the boxes on the carpet in between us all.

Being a mom, and having an obligation to embarrass me, she sat down next to Jason and folded her short, now jean-clad legs underneath her, then she began quizzing Max and Jason. I sat back down on Jason's other side with a sigh. Jason watched the embarrassment grow on my face, smiling, and answered all of my mom's inane questions politely. I kept my eyes on my pizza, trying not to frown.

At one point my mom pulled her pale blue tank top straight, going into business mode, and asked to see our school project. We told her we were still in the "brainstorming stage" and she let it go. Forty-five excruciating minutes later, she decided that her embarrassing mom requirement for the week had been achieved. She grabbed the empty pizza boxes and left us to "get back to work."

When conversation began to run out, the topic came to me and the whole "non-human" thing.

"So what are the possibilities?" Allison asked Jason.

Jason glanced at me, then answered, "There are many supernatural creatures that can produce offspring with humans, some more rare than others. Many people have elven blood without even knowing it. Full blooded elves are extremely rare these days, mainly because their bloodlines have become almost completely entwined with humans."

"Could that be what I am?" I interrupted hopefully. Elves didn't sound too bad.

Jason shook his head, dashing my hopes. "You may have some elven blood, but Max and I would not be able to smell the difference. Your non-human blood is something much more rare."

I sighed, getting crabby. "Spit it out already."

Jason went on, "One option is Ogres, but I doubt that's what you are, you would likely be much larger. Another one is Merpeople."

"Merpeople?" Allison asked incredulously.

Jason regarded her. "Merpeople have two forms. When under water, they are in their natural form, very similar to the common depiction of mermaids. On land, they look much like humans, except for the second eyelids. For some reason, those remain even in human form."

Okay, Merpeople were slightly more unsettling than elves, but again, not horrible. "What are my chances of that?"

"Pretty good," Jason replied. "Merpeople are a great deal more common than one would think."

I nodded, taking it all in. "Any other options?"

Jason hesitated. He ran his hand through his hair. Not a good sign. Finally, he spoke. "The last option that I came up with was . . . demons."

My heart skipped a beat. I swallowed past the lump in my throat. "Seriously?"

He nodded and answered, "It's not as uncommon as you would think. Demons often mate with humans, producing half-demons. Demons can look like humans, as can merpeople and ogres. Your mom probably thought your dad was just a normal guy."

"What about werewolves?" Lucy chimed in.

Jason shook his head, "We can rule out werewolves, vampires, or any conditions resulting from being cursed. All can produce offspring with humans, but none can pass on their afflictions."

I held my breath at Jason's mention of vampires, waiting for Lucy or Allison to question him further on the subject. Surprisingly, they both seemed to take the mention of vampires in stride.

Lucy nodded in response to Jason's answer. "Well that's something at least."

So, I could be an ogre (unlikely), a mermaid (not so bad), or . . . a demon (gulp). That seemingly ever-present feeling of dread had returned to the pit of my stomach ten-fold. Like Lucy said, at least we could rule out werewolf and vampire, which also meant that I had my answer about how Jason became a vampire. Small consolation, that.

As we were finishing that lovely subject, I glanced at the clock. 9:00 pm, time for the boys to "leave." They were going to leave out the front door and drive Jason's car to hide it. Then they would walk back to my house, do a perimeter check, and sneak back in through my window. When I asked how they were going to climb in through my second-story window, they both smiled mischievously and walked out of my room. I guess we'd find out.

The boys' departure was Allison's cue for girl talk.

"So Xoe," she started, "pray tell, what is going on between you and Jason?" She smiled wickedly at me.

I gave her my best dumbfounded look. "What? Nothing, why do you ask?"

Allison sighed, "Oh, come on. Don't play dumb, you two are *so* obvious."

With a sigh of my own, I answered, "Nothing Allison, just friends."

"And why is that?" she went on. "Is it the whole vampire thing?"

My jaw dropped. How did Allison know?

She smiled. "Max told us."

That little rat . . . I mean wolf. Well, at least I wasn't the last to know. "So what if it is the vampire thing?" I replied.

Allison crossed her arms and looked at me as if I were being childish. "Who cares? It's not like he kills people anymore. He's one of the good guys now."

I sighed loudly. "Emphasis on the *now*. The fact still remains that he killed people at one time, and who even said I was interested in him to begin with?"

"Pah-lease, I see the way you watch him," Allison countered. "And there is definitely no mistaking the way he watches you."

At that we all turned to a knock at the window. Apparently the boys had finished their perimeter check. Thankfully, the girl talk could end. I stood and opened the window for them to climb in.

"The way who watches who?" Max asked as he

pulled himself in. They really *had* climbed all the way up to my two-story window, though I wasn't sure how. The storm drain maybe?

Really, I was more concerned with how much of our conversation they'd heard. The three of us girls crossed our arms and stared Max down with our best stern faces. He shrugged off our glares and plopped down on my bed as Jason climbed in through the window after him.

Turning my attention away from Max, I asked Jason, "Anything to report?"

He shook his head. "Not much, we caught Dan's scent in a few places around the yard, so he's been here recently, but nothing looked out of place."

I nodded. There was a knock at the door. I quickly hustled the boys into the closet, then yelled, "Come in!"

My mom peeked her head in to see that we were all accounted for and told us goodnight. She closed the door softly, oblivious to our nervous smiles and murmured goodnights.

Since most of us were going on little to no sleep, we decided to sleep in shifts. Allison, Lucy, and I all changed into pajamas, while the boys chose to remain in the clothes they had worn during the day. I chose to wear a dark purple cami with matching purple plaid pajama pants, as opposed to my usual t-shirt and boxers. I refused to admit to myself that I did it because Jason was there.

Allison and Jason had first watch. Lucy and I took the bed, snuggling under my fluffy green comforter. Max was left with an orange sleeping bag on the floor. Jason turned on my desk lamp, then turned off the overhead light. I shut my eyes with a silent wish for normal dreams void of fire, and I was out.

13

I woke up to loud ringing. My alarm clock. That meant it was 6:00 am. When blindly smacking it didn't seem to quell the alarm's desire to annoy me, I ripped the cord out of the wall. I sat up, rubbing my eyes and looked blearily around my room. What were all of these people doing in here? My eyes landed on Jason, who had his hand over his mouth, trying not to laugh at me. Oh yeah, Jason, Max, werewolves, vampires . . . I remembered now. Jason managed to cover his smile, but his eyes still shone with humor.

"Glad to be amusing," I mumbled at him.

I looked around to the other people in my room. Lucy and Allison had managed to ignore my alarm, and were still snuggled in bed with me. Max wasn't so lucky. He struggled out of his sleeping bag and stumbled into the bathroom, shutting the door noisily. I looked back to Jason.

"I'll drive you all to school today," he said.

I nodded sleepily, and got out of bed to find something to wear. Jason watched me as I shuffled through the shirts hanging in my closet, finally settling on a plain, dark gray tee shirt with a faded *Star Wars* logo on the front. I was searching for a clean pair of jeans when Max came back out of the bathroom. He walked toward the window, unlatched it, pushed it open, then hopped, and I mean *hopped*, out of my second-story window. Yeah, I wasn't getting used to this supernatural stuff anytime soon.

Jason spared me a final smile then followed Max's lead. I walked to the window and looked out at the ground. Max and Jason were already out of sight. Too weird.

I returned to the bed and shook Allison and Lucy awake, much to their chagrin. We all took speed-showers and got dressed. A cold gust of wind from the still open window reminded me to throw on my forest-green hoodie, then I watched Allison while she was putting on her make-up. She was dressed in a sea foam green blouse that was kind of draped in the front, I've never known what those types of blouses are called, and a beige mini-skirt with knee high, dark brown leather boots. I asked her if Jason had been the one to keep watch all night.

"Vampires don't sleep," was her reply. Ask a silly question.

We went downstairs into the kitchen, heading

straight for the coffee maker. My mom had left me half of a pot. I filled my travel mug with as much as it would hold, then went to the pantry to find something for us to eat on the way to school. Looked like it was granola bars for breakfast again. I handed one each to Lucy and Allison and stuffed my own into the front pocket of my hoodie.

We went out the front door to find Jason's car waiting to take us to school. I snagged the front seat without protest from Lucy and Allison. I could feel them watching and waiting to see how I would interact with Jason. I wanted to stare ga-ga-eyed at him, but wouldn't give them the satisfaction. Girlfriends . . . can't live with 'em, can't live without 'em. At the moment I was leaning toward without. I contented myself with watching him out of the corner of my eye. He was still in his clothes from the day before, but the t-shirt looked so good on him, that I didn't really mind. I placed my travel mug into one of the cup-holders and slowly began to unwrap my granola bar, refusing to be the first one to make conversation. Jason put the car in drive, and away we went.

The short drive was spent mostly in silence. I fiddled with the radio, just for something to do, scanning through the few radio stations that come in clearly in Shelby. As soon as we pulled up to the school, Allison and Lucy practically leapt from the car, leaving me alone with Jason. It seemed a planned move, and probably was. Sigh.

"What's the plan for today?" I asked him.

He turned his attention to me. "I am going to wait around the school and make sure Dan doesn't get to Lucy without me or Max there. I'll pick you all up when you get out."

"You aren't coming to class?"

Jason smiled and shook his head. "I am not exactly a student."

That reminded me of another question I had for him. "How did you manage to register and get into my English class anyways?"

"I mustn't reveal all my secrets," he answered, wiggling his eyebrows at me.

I gave him a good-natured smirk, then got out of the car with a smile that I simply could not help.

I went to my first class, and the day went by slowly from there. By lunchtime there was still no sign of Dan. I met up with Allison and Lucy and we sat at our usual table. "Anything to report?" I asked them.

They both gave me mischievous smiles. "We were going to ask you the same question," said Allison.

I gave them wide eyes.

"What did you and Jason talk about?" Lucy interjected, smiling from ear to ear.

"We simply discussed the matter at hand, nothing more," I answered with my nose up. My denial did nothing to dampen their knowing smiles. Time for a subject change.

I looked at Lucy. "How are you feeling today? Do you feel any . . . different?"

Lucy thought in silence for a moment, unconsciously straightening her pale purple sweater, then answered, "I don't know. I keep looking for changes, but I feel pretty much the same. Max said that my senses would increase, but I haven't noticed. I guess it just takes time. What about you? Have you come up with any ideas about your 'mysterious origin'?"

I sighed. "Let's not even go there. I haven't had any time to think about it. Even if I did, I don't see how I'd be able to figure anything out on my own."

Allison and Lucy both looked down at the table.

Allison turned her eyes back up to me. "You could always ask your mom. Maybe tell her you want to track down your dad, just to meet him. All you need is his name. We can track him down and ask him ourselves."

I sighed again. "I guess we can try, I doubt my mom will give me his name. She likes to pretend that he never existed. If I would believe it, she'd probably try and tell me that I was a test-tube baby or something. Plus, I'm not really sure I'd *want* to meet him, even if it was just to get answers."

It was my turn to look down at the off-white table. I tried to distract myself by reading the various things that people had carved into the tabletop over the years. I traced my finger over a star that was carved deeply into the wood. Our school was either too cheap to buy new tables, or else they were smart enough to know that the new ones would be carved up within weeks. Curse that teenage angst.

"So what's the plan after school today? Another slumber party?" Allison asked, regaining my attention.

Allison can stay over whenever she feels like it. Her parents don't really place many rules and restrictions on her. She pretty much does whatever she wants.

Glad to have the subject off of me again, I answered, "All I know is that Jason is picking us up after school. He said that he was going to try to find out what Dan is up to, so I guess that will govern what our plan will be."

Lucy looked worried. "I don't think my parents will let me stay away another night, and it's doubtful they will let anyone stay over either."

Hmm, quandary. "I don't know," I said. "We'll figure something out."

The bell rang. It was time for gym, the one bright spot, besides lunchtime, in my day. Allison and I said goodbye to Lucy then headed to the gymnasium.

According to Mitch the plan for gym today was a *free day*. Free day? What the heck was a free day? Mitch's gym teacher license should have been revoked long ago. Allison was all smiles after Mitch announced that we could do whatever we wanted with our gym period, as long as it was P.E. Related, of course. Allison and I went into the locker room and changed into our gym clothes.

As we left the locker room we were joined by a

suspicious looking Brian. He looked down at me with squinted eyes, "You care to elaborate Ma'm?" he asked me as he crossed his arms, looking very detective-like.

I answered snarkily, "What *are* you talking about Brian?"

He continued, "You know what I mean. What were those guys doing at your house yesterday? Did you suddenly decide to expand your circle of friends?"

I nodded, smiling sweetly.

He continued, "No, doubtful, very doubtful. Hmmm, let me guess again. You're involved in a random conspiracy concerning aliens, and that Jason character is a rogue FBI agent out to reveal the truth to the public. Yep, that sounds a lot more likely than Alexondra Meyers trying to make new friends."

Ok, so he obviously was not going to let it go. With a resigned sigh, I explained, "We've been having some trouble with that new guy, Dan, and Jason and Max have been hanging around to make sure that he doesn't bother us, that's all."

Brian looked hurt. "Why didn't you ask me? I *do* live right next door, and I should hope that you trust me more than some guy you've hardly ever spoken to and some guy you just met."

I hadn't considered that when I fabricated my lie. In an effort to soothe his hurt feelings, I lied some more. "Lucy's dating Max, so Max volunteered to watch out for us. Max brought Jason along to help out."

Allison gave me an 'are you crazy?' look. Yeah, so

I'm not the greatest liar around. Shouldn't that be a good thing? I just had to hope that Lucy wouldn't find out, or I'd be in for a major lecture.

Brian was not so easily sated, he continued, "Jason seemed awful possessive of you to be just a random friend that Max brought with him. He was practically guarding your heels the whole time I was there."

I was out of lies, so I feigned ignorance instead, "Oh, um, I hadn't noticed."

Brian didn't look like he believed me, but he let it go. I had a feeling that the subject had only been dropped temporarily. Brian grabbed a basketball and looked at me, then nodded toward the unoccupied hoop. Brian and I went to play *one-on-one* while Allison watched.

The rest of the day went by too quickly for my taste. I never thought I'd see the day when I would be reluctant to go home from school. The end of the school day meant that our focus had to go back to werewolf matters.

Allison and I left our last class and headed toward the school entrance to find Lucy waiting just inside the doors, rather than outside like she usually did. I was glad to see that she was being cautious. I linked my arm with hers and the three of us headed to the parking lot to meet our fate.

14

Jason was waiting in the lot for us, sitting casually on the hood of his fancy-schmancy car. He was dressed in black pants, a charcoal colored wool coat, and a dark blue, button up shirt that brought out the deep blue of his eyes. His hair was in tousled disarray, as usual, contrasting with his clean-cut clothes.

Jason smiled a crooked smile as we approached. He hopped to his feet to unlock the driver's side door . . . or so I thought. Instead he walked around to the front passenger side and held the door open, looking at me expectantly.

Huh? "What, am I driving or something?" I asked.

"No, I am." He just stood there smiling.

I stared at him dumbly. Jason sighed and gestured with his hand to still empty passenger seat. I walked slowly toward the car and stood to face him, still not understanding . . . okay, so maybe I'm a little slow at times. He stepped back from the door and continued to smile at me, though there was a hint of nervous impatience in it now. I turned my back to him and slid into the car tentatively. He gently shut the door behind me and went back around to the driver's side.

Lucy and Allison had both slid into the back seat during the exchange. I looked at them to find wicked grins plastered across their faces. I would never hear the end of this. Never.

Jason slid into the driver's seat and shut his door behind him. He looked quite pleased with himself, the nerves gone. I wasn't sure if the act of chivalry was sincere or if it was a joke. I wasn't sure I wanted to know.

Jason started the car and pulled out. We drove in silence in the direction of my house. Playing my usual role of awkward silence-breaker, I asked Jason, "Did you find anything out today?"

He spared a quick glance away from the road for me, then turning back, answered, "I couldn't detect any sign of Dan. His scent is all over town, but it doesn't lead anywhere away from Shelby. My guess is that he either drove out of town, or is hiding somewhere. I'm leaning toward the latter. He does not intend to leave without Lucy."

Allison leaned her head between Jason and me, honey blonde hair hanging forward over her shoulders. "So what? We just have to wait for him to come get us?"

Jason kept his eyes on the road while he answered, "Max is out trying to pinpoint Dan's hiding place. I will be staying with the three of you in case he tries to come for Lucy."

I crossed my arms and pouted. "Why do you get to be the one to stay with us, while Max has to traipse all over town?" So maybe I was a little grumpy about the stunt Jason had pulled with the door. Can you blame me? I still wasn't sure whether or not he was playing a joke on me.

He gave me a slightly offended look. "Max has a much better sense of smell than I do, and I have a much better chance of protecting you against Dan than Max does."

Couldn't argue with that logic, though I wanted to.

We pulled into my driveway and got out of the car.

"Where's your mom?" Lucy asked me.

"I forgot that she's off doing some study on birds in Washington today, luckily, so we don't have to worry about coming up with another excuse to have everybody over."

I walked to unlock the door and Jason came to stand next to me, first in line to go inside. He insisted on going in ahead of us in case Dan was waiting in ambush. He walked in and started checking all of the rooms for any sign of foul play.

I walked into the kitchen, leaving Allison and Lucy

in the living room to watch TV. My mom had left money for pizza on the kitchen counter with a note that said as much. The note also specifically stated that I was not to have boys over while she was gone. Too late on that one. Ah well, as the cliché goes, what she doesn't know, can't hurt her. The list of things that I had to hide from my mom seemed to be growing exponentially of late. I felt a little sad about that. I was used to sharing almost everything with her.

I grabbed the portable phone out of its cradle on the wall and called Irvine's to order two extra large pizzas: one pepperoni, and one mushroom. Jason walked into the kitchen behind me as I was hanging up the phone. I looked away from him and noticed that the potted African violet in the window looked a little dry. I grabbed it off of the sill and put it under the faucet to give it some water, ignoring Jason's presence.

"All clear?" I asked, not looking up. I saw him nod out of the corner of my eye, watching me with his arms crossed. "What?" I asked grumpily, setting down the plant and looking directly at him.

"Did I do something wrong? You seem . . . hostile."

Sighing, I asked, "What was that stunt with the door about? Did you do it just to embarrass me?"

Jason looked taken aback. He stared at me wide-eyed for a moment before answering, "Isn't that what a guy's supposed to do, when, you know, he's trying to woo a girl?"

Woo? He was trying to *woo* me? I was too amused

to remain angry. I tried to contain my laughter and failed. "Um, not that I've ever been *wooed*, but I'm perfectly capable of opening my own doors. Who gave you permission to woo me anyhow?"

He looked at me with a stubborn set to his jaw. "Well I am sorry that you have never been wooed, but it has been a *very* long time since I have done the wooing. I cannot be expected to get it right on my first try."

I started laughing again, there was just no holding it in. Jason crossed his arms and tried to stare me down with a petulant look on his face. I kept laughing. When he began to realize the ridiculousness of the situation, he let that crooked smile of his slowly appear on his face, then he began to laugh along with me. Soon we were both laughing so hard we couldn't breathe.

"What is going on here?" Allison interrupted. She had walked into the kitchen to stand in front of Jason and me with her arms crossed, tapping her foot on the tile floor like an angry parent.

"Woo!" I exclaimed, tears streaming down my face, doubling Jason's and my laughter. Allison made a noise of exasperation and walked back into the living room with her hands in the air. Our laughter began to slowly die down, and we were left grinning at each other.

"I'm sorry," I said. "It was a very nice attempt at wooing."

"Oh, no," Jason replied sarcastically, "there is no

salvaging it now." He turned and walked out of the kitchen toward the living room, still grinning.

I stayed in the kitchen a minute longer, trying to control the smile on my face. Mustn't get feelings for the vampire. Yeah Xoe, keep telling yourself that.

I looked out the window and caught sight of Brian, clothed in gray sweats, getting home from football practice. He had to walk home just like us other unfortunates without cars. He paused in his driveway, noticing Jason's car parked in my driveway. He gave the car a less than friendly look and went into his house.

Frowning, I went to join the others in the living room.

Allison had pulled out several board games and laid them out on the coffee table. "Pick your poison," she told Lucy and Jason. Before they could answer, Allison turned to acknowledge me. "What's wrong?" she asked, taking in my lugubrious expression.

I shook my head ruefully. "Nothing. I vote for *Scrabble.*"

Allison grabbed the scrabble box and started setting up the board on the coffee table. Lucy began turning all of the little letter tiles upside-down in the box since we'd long ago lost the bag they were supposed to go in.

"Max is here," Jason said an instant before Max knocked on the door.

I walked to the door and let him inside. "Did you find anything?" I asked.

Max shook his head. "Dan's been everywhere. He's crisscrossed his scent all over the place. I can't find a definite trail."

Jason chimed in, "That's what I expected. He's hiding out, waiting for an opportunity to strike."

"Um," Max began, "I found something else."

We all looked to Max expectantly.

"Other scents. There are other wolves in town."

"Could it be Dan's old pack, trying to find him?" I asked.

"I don't think so," Jason answered. "Packs don't travel much. They don't want to risk crossing into another pack's territory. That's why they hired me." He paused to think for a moment. "Could you tell how many?"

"Two, besides Dan," Max answered. "At least, that's how many I caught scent of."

"What do we do?" I asked.

"We do all we can do," Jason replied. "Wait."

So it looked like we would have to wait for Dan, and maybe others, to come to us. Gotta love a stake-out . . . or not.

I started to shut the door behind Max, but noticed Brian coming our way. I swear, he was worse than a puppy. I went outside and shut the door behind me. I had a feeling that a confrontation was in my near future. Brian stomped toward me, looking angry. He'd changed into a plain white t-shirt and jeans.

He stopped right in front of me, arms crossed. "I've

been thinking about your story Xoe, and I have to say, I don't believe a word of it. We've been friends a long time, and if you're in some sort of trouble, I deserve to know. I can help." He gave me a slightly pleading look that was overtaken by his anger within seconds.

I didn't know why he was so angry. I mean, I could understand him being a little jealous about being left out, but this amount of anger was uncalled for. Men are always saying how difficult women are to understand, but they hadn't met the men in my life, they could give any woman a run for her money.

I stared at him blankly, considering my answer, then words tumbled out of my mouth. "Trouble's over. Dan left town, Jason and Max just came over to hang out."

Brian did not look convinced, but I hadn't really expected him to be. He roughly ran his hand through his hair in a frustrated gesture, making his short curls puff up. He said coldly, "You've always been a terrible liar Xoe."

Matching him stare for stare, I answered just as coldly, "What do you want me to say?"

Brian shook his head and swept past me, going for the door. My guilt turned quickly into anger. I didn't owe him any explanation! How dare he! I ran after him and caught up as he was reaching for the doorknob.

I reached out and grabbed his wrist before he could turn the knob. Things seemed to go in slow motion. He jerked away from me with a yelp of pain. I looked at him dumbly, confused by his reaction. Then I saw his arm. A blistery burn, roughly the size of my hand, circled his wrist. I stared at him confused. My vision began to go dark. The last thing I saw was the terrified look on Brian's face. Terrified of me. Then the ground came up to meet me.

I woke to dark blue eyes above me. Wait, hadn't this happened before? The eyes disappeared for a moment, then I felt Jason pulling me into his lap. He leaned me against his chest so I could sit upright. My limbs ached with flu-like weakness. I couldn't move. My vision faded in and out. Jason ran his hands up and down my arms, like you do when you're trying to warm someone up.

We were outside my front door. Lucy, Allison, and Max had all come outside as well. Brian was standing a safe distance away, cradling his wrist.

"We had to fill him in on some stuff," Allison said, nodding in Brian's direction. Allison looked uneasy. She seemed afraid to get too close to the situation. I looked at Brian's face. His face was set in angry lines, but his eyes held unmistakable fear.

Brian stared back at me, unable to make his face completely impassive, though I could tell that's what he was trying to go for. "I just wanted to make sure you were okay before I left. I don't want any part of—this. Whatever *this* is. I get the point. I'll leave you alone from now on. You didn't have to burn me."

My mouth fell open. I tried to speak and my voice

cracked. I tried again with a little more success, "I-I didn't mean to. I don't know what happened."

Brian didn't answer. He just turned and walked away toward his house.

Jason stood, lifting me up in his arms, and carried me inside. He laid me down gently on the couch as I heard the footsteps of the others following us.

Allison and Lucy came to hover beside me. I heard someone, Max, by process of elimination, shut and lock the door. Max walked up to stand beside Jason.

Allison looked in their direction. "Could we have a little privacy?"

Nodding and mumbling uncomfortably, the boys unlocked the door again and went back outside. The noises that came from their exit: the hushed tones of their voices, their footsteps, the click of the door shutting, all seemed like a distant dream to me. Allison lifted me up partially so that she could sit down and lay my head in her lap. She started stroking my hair, trying to be comforting.

"What happened Xoe?" she asked.

Lucy sat on the floor and grabbed my hand. Hot tears stung my eyes. I tried to stop them, but they flowed faster and faster. What *had* happened?

"I hurt Brian. I don't know how, but I did." My tears were a mixture of confusion and fear. "He's one of my oldest friends and . . . and . . ." My words caught in my throat. "He's afraid of me!" The tears turned into raking sobs. I hiccuped on my breaths, trying to draw in enough air and failing.

It was just too much. I had managed to keep my cool through everything that had happened, but this was just *too* much. My friends held me, Allison with my head in her lap and Lucy clinging to my hand, as I cried out my frustration and fear. Underneath the frustration and fear was an immense sadness. A sadness in knowing that life as I knew it had changed—forever. I had always had a solid sense of who I was . . . what I was. Now everything felt like quicksand. I was being sucked under into a new world, a new me.

When my tears had quieted, Jason and Max came back inside. They had probably heard the whole thing with their supernatural ears, but I was still grateful for the illusion of privacy they had given me. I looked at them, eyes red and puffy, and asked, "What's happening to me?"

Jason knelt beside Lucy. "I think you are coming into your powers. Nothing like this has ever happened before?"

I shook my head.

He continued, "If this is just starting now, we can expect more powers to manifest, or for this one to grow in strength." Jason averted his eyes.

I stared at him until he gave in and met my gaze. "What aren't you telling me?"

Jason's eyes held mine steadily. "This type of power is usually related to . . . demons."

My eyes widened. Even if I could make sense of my friends being werewolves and vampires, I could *not* comprehend being a demon. Jason had told me that it was a possibility, but I hadn't allowed myself to think too hard on it.

"Elaborate," I said shakily.

"Well," he began, "out of our three options, demons are the only ones that possess this type of destructive power. Merpeople are capable of a mild amount of enchantment, and Ogres are simply strong. The powers of demons tend to be more . . . obvious."

I had an awful idea. "So . . . am I like, bad?" I asked, not sure I really wanted to know. I noticed Lucy dart a worried look up at Allison.

Jason answered, "No, as far as I know, the manifestation of your genetics is often dependent on your upbringing. Demons have an inborn tendency toward violence and rage, but they do not have to act on their impulses. You were raised like a human, and therefore think like one . . . You simply need to watch your temper."

I looked a question at him.

He went on, "Demons are marked by their anger. I believe that is what your powers are linked to. You burned Brian because you were angry."

The room was spinning. I had to focus. I held perfectly still, breathing deeply, trying to not let things sink in until I had gotten all of the facts. "What other 'powers'" I gulped, "can I expect?"

"I am not certain. There are different types of demons. Their powers vary. Given that the first power you exerted was to burn someone, your abilities will likely be linked to fire."

Fire? That could explain the dreams. I reached my hand up to pinch the bridge of my nose. I had a major headache building behind my eyes. "How do you know all this?"

He looked down briefly, then met my eyes. "I have suspected that you were most likely a half-demon since the beginning. I did some research, called some friends who are a little more knowledgeable on this type of thing. Half-demons are the most common human hybrid, more so than Merpeople and Ogres. Any other races that can breed with humans are either very rare or gone altogether."

The room was still spinning. I closed my eyes to quell my dizziness. "Did your knowledgeable friends give you any other information?"

Jason lightly placed his hand on the shoulder that I wasn't lying on. "I'm sorry Xoe, I've told you all that I know."

I was overwhelmed, even with this scant amount of information. "What do we do now?" I asked, clinging to my last thread of hope. Maybe it wouldn't be such a big deal. Maybe the "powers" would stop here. Maybe they would just go away. And maybe the moon is made of cheese to feed the little green men.

Jason replied, "There's not much that we can do. As

your powers come, *if* your powers come, you will learn to control them."

That sounded like a lot of trial and error to me. I'd already hurt one friend. I shuddered at the thought of the damage I might do before I got things under control, *if* I got things under control. It was a very big if.

"Is there anything else I should know?" I asked, not really knowing what I was asking for, as Jason had already said all that he knew. The panic was coming back. I closed my eyes and tried to slow my breathing, afraid I was going to hyperventilate and pass out again.

Jason answered, "Probably, but like I said, I have told you all that I know."

Angry and frustrated I replied, "Well, then I guess we should just focus on Dan and the matter at hand."

No one argued with the sharpness of my words. Each person nodded his or her assent. I knew there was no way I was going to be able to focus on anything except my recent horrifying news, but I needed the subject off me. I had a lot of processing to do and no time to do it in. A girl's troubles never end.

15

We spent the rest of the afternoon playing scrabble, eating pizza, and trying to ignore what we had discovered about me. I'm usually pretty good at scrabble, but today I was filling up the board with three-letter words. The pizza guy had been really late, which I guess was good, considering what he could have walked in on. Plus, we got the order for free. My first slice was still sitting abandoned on a paper plate next to me. When we got bored of scrabble, we resorted to watching a movie.

I couldn't focus on the TV screen. I looked around at my living room and the people that currently inhabited it. Jason, Max, and Allison were sharing the larger dark blue couch that I had been lying on when I'd had my breakdown. Jason and Allison each clung to their respective corners while Max lounged in the center. I greedily hogged the mismatched purple love seat. I needed distance, mentally and physically, to absorb all that had happened. Lucy lay on her stomach on the purple, blue, and green patchwork rug that covered the living room floor, using a throw pillow to prop herself up. My mom had gotten the rug to try and tie in the colors of our two couches, emphasis on the word *try*.

I hugged a green throw pillow, clutching it against my stomach. For the past few hours my body had been debating whether I was going to pass out, throw up, or scream. Maybe a little bit of each, hopefully not simultaneously. My worry had been building a solid knot in my gut. What had started life as a golf ball of fear and worry had grown to bowling ball proportions. The more I thought about everything, the less sense it all made.

For lack of any better distractions, I grabbed my mom's most recent *National Geographic* and went into the dining room. I pulled out a chair, sat down, and started leafing through the pages of the magazine, not really looking at them.

Lucy came into the dining room shortly after me and sat down on one of the high-backed maple chairs that matched the table. She nervously fiddled with a yellow woven placemat.

She smiled weakly at me. "No offense Xoe, but . . . I'm kind of glad you're a half-demon."

I gave her a 'you're kidding,' look. She was . . . glad?

She went on, "Not that you're a demon specifically,

it's just nice that I'm not the only newly non-human one. I was feeling pretty alone."

"Well I guess when you put it that way, I'm pretty glad you're a werewolf," I replied.

Lucy smiled, a little more strongly this time. "Thanks for everything Xoe. I mean it. If it weren't for you I'd be curled up in a ball crying right now . . . or maybe worse."

You would think that at a moment like this Lucy would give me a hug, grab my hand, or even just pat my shoulder, just . . . something. However, Lucy kept her distance, hands neatly folded on the table. I had a feeling she wasn't as comfortable with things as she was trying to put off. It wasn't every day you found out that your best friend came from demonic origins.

I gave her a forced smile. "Glad to be of service." My own best friend was afraid of me. She was a were-wolf, and she was afraid of me.

We were weakly smiling at each other when Allison walked into the dining room to join us. She whined, "Do you both realize that now I'm the only measly human left? It's so unfair. You get all these cool superpowers and I'm still just the same old me."

Lucy and I burst into laughter, releasing some of the tension. Allison crossed her arms and pouted, plopping down in the chair next to Lucy. She'd get over it. I wasn't sure I would.

I glanced out the wide dining room window. The

sun was making its descent, giving way to darkness. Clouds obscured most of what light was left.

Lucy stood. "I guess I should call my parents."

"You think they'll let you stay over?" Allison asked.

Lucy shook her head lugubriously and trudged into the kitchen to retrieve the phone. Allison and I waited in silence in order to listen to Lucy's end of the conversation, short as it was. Lucy hung up the phone and came back to face us.

"No?" I asked, already knowing the answer.

Lucy shook her head.

"Jason!" I called.

Jason came trotting into the dining room, leaving Max alone in the living room. "Yes?"

I sighed. "Lucy can't stay. What do we do?"

Jason sat down across from me in Lucy's vacated chair. "In all likelihood, Dan will expect us to stick together. He will check here first, since we have spent most of our time here. I will wait here for Dan. Xoe, you and Allison are going to leave now and hide at my hotel. Lucy will go back to her house long enough for her parents to go to sleep, then Max will help her sneak out so that they can go to my hotel as well. Once you are all together, you will drive. I want you to stay on the move until I call you on Max's cell phone."

I rolled my eyes at Jason. "That's the *dumbest* plan I've ever heard."

Jason looked at me, stunned.

I went on, "We're not leaving you here alone to

fight Dan. We've already established that he might have other wolves with him. You'll get yourself killed and then we'll be back to square one, only with one less person to help keep us *all* alive."

Jason glared at me. "I can take care of myself, I won't risk you . . . any of you."

I smiled haughtily. "Well seeing as this is my house, you can't very well kick me out. I'm staying and you have no choice in the matter."

Max chimed in, "I'm not human. I can help."

Jason turned to Allison. "And how do you feel about all of this?"

Allison raised her nose in the air, signaling that there were to be no arguments. "I'm staying with either Xoe or Lucy, preferably both. I'm not going to hide out."

We all looked at Lucy. I asked, "Do you think you'll be able to sneak out?"

Lucy looked down and shook her head, then forced her gaze to meet mine. "You know how my parents are. They check on me throughout the night. I don't know what they would do if I were missing, probably call the cops."

Jason stood, a little angrily. "So you all refuse to hide?"

"You got it," Allison answered.

Jason crossed his arms and glared at me. I smiled back sweetly, sure of myself. Finally, Jason gave one quick nod in agreement. "Fine, new plan. Dan will still likely check here first, so I will still wait here. We have already established that Lucy has to stay at her house, so Max will sneak in and wait with her." He turned to once again regard Allison and me. "As for you two, since you insist on putting yourselves in more danger, you can place yourselves at either house, but I would prefer it if you stayed with me. Max needs to concentrate on keeping Lucy safe and I will have a better chance of protecting you."

I had to point out the obvious flaw. "What if Dan goes to Lucy's first?"

"If Max catches scent of Dan, he will call us here from his cell phone."

Jason looked to Max as Max nodded his agreement.

It was a plan I could live with, and hopefully I would. I slapped my hands together and said dramatically, "It's a plan then, C'mon folks we're burnin' daylight!"

We all went together in Jason's car to take Lucy and Max down the street to Lucy's house. I watched Lucy go in through her front door and couldn't help thinking that it might be the last time I ever saw her. Who could really say what would happen? I felt tears stinging my eyes for the second time that day. On the drive back to my place, I began to have some serious doubts. At least, more serious than the thousands I already had.

"Are you sure you can take on Dan?" I asked Jason, "I mean, maybe we should have the same plan as Lucy and Max. If you smell him coming, call Max over to help."

"We can't risk leaving Lucy alone," Jason replied. "Dan is stronger than Max, but having Max there is still better than the alternatives."

There was something else that had been chewing at the back of my mind all night. Jason had managed to skim over it when I had brought it up earlier. "What about the other wolves that Max smelled? What if they're with Dan?"

Jason did not look happy. "There is nothing we can do about that. We just have to hope for the best."

Comforting, very comforting. "I think this is a really bad idea."

Jason sighed and kept his eyes on the road. "So do I."

What could I say?

Once we returned to my house, the three of us went inside and inspected the premises to make sure all of the doors and windows were locked. Then we sat down in the living room to wait. Allison and I squished onto the love seat while Jason sat on the end of the couch closest to us. Our plan really wasn't a plan at all. We were leaving things completely up to chance, and the chance of success was slim.

"Should we have weapons?" I asked Jason.

"I'm more efficient without weapons," Jason replied, "but I suppose it couldn't hurt for you and Allison to be armed."

Allison leaned over the coffee table to rifle through her purse. She pulled out a canister of pepper spray, holding it up for Jason's approval.

He shrugged. "It's better than nothing."

I got up and grabbed the poker from our set of fireplace tools and sat back down with it across my lap. Jason and Allison both raised an eyebrow at me. I shrugged. Better than nothing.

After about thirty minutes of Al and me jumping at every sound, Jason voiced that we should get some sleep. After all, we weren't even sure that Dan would come. The three of us went up to my room. Allison and I snuggled up in my bed, while Jason sat at my desk chair and kept watch. I closed my eyes and tried to sleep, fireplace poker gripped tightly in my hands. Call it paranoia. I called it survival.

16

It felt like I had just fallen asleep when I was awakened by a loud crash downstairs. We all sprung up and thundered downstairs into the living room with our "weapons" to find Dan waiting . . . and he brought a friend. A willowy, tall woman with long dark glossy hair stood to Dan's right. Her features and deep olive skin were exotic, though I couldn't quite place them to a specific nationality. She wore tight black jeans and a matching shirt. Dan's pale blue eyes held malice. The woman looked uneasy. Dan matched the woman in dress: black jeans and t-shirt. The monochromatic duo come to call.

Glass shards littered the ground where Dan had broken the window next to my front door. Large spears of glass still remained in the pane. He had only needed a hole big enough for him to reach through and unlock the door. I was surprised that he had chosen to break into the front. He was either very bold or very stupid, or maybe he just didn't care. I was betting on the latter.

If the woman was a wolf, which I was guessing she was, we were over-matched, at least I thought we were. To tell the truth, I had no idea how two werewolves, one of unknown power and the other apparently pretty powerful, matched up with a vampire, a human, and a half-demon just come into her powers. We were about to find out.

Jason dove for Dan, not waiting for him to make the first move. They tumbled behind the blue couch, partially out of sight, leaving Allison and me to deal with the woman.

She rushed us, long hair streaming behind her. Allison whipped her hand up holding the pepper spray. She sprayed the woman in the face, but other than pinching her eyes shut in pain, it didn't seem to faze her. It didn't even slow her charge. She rushed on, grabbing Allison and throwing her against the wall behind us, next to the stairs. Allison hit the wall with a thud, then slid to the floor like a rag doll, going frighteningly still.

I stood, jaw gaping, staring at Allison's still form. My pulse thundered in my ears, blocking out all other sound. I turned back to our assailant.

The skin around the woman's eyes was red and swollen. She squinted at me, trying to see through her puffy eyelids, but didn't seem to notice the pain anymore. So apparently pepper spray did have some effect on werewolves, just not as much of an effect as we'd hoped.

The woman began stalking toward me, crouched in some sort of fighter's stance. Her movements were liquid grace. I darted a nervous glance to see Jason and Dan grappling on the floor. Jason seemed to be losing. His body was mostly obscured from my vision by Dan's broad back. I watched in horror as Dan raised a hand that had sprouted claws. The fingers had gotten thicker, each tip dominated by a long, black claw. The hand had grown wider into a rounded square shape. The mutated hand dove down at Jason's chest.

I ripped my gaze away and forced my attention back to my opponent. She sniffed the air and looked at me as she cocked her head, perplexed. She still stood in her fighter's crouch, hands clenching and unclenching, weighing her odds. It took every ounce of my self-restraint not to run to Jason. A low growl tricked out of the woman's rose-petal mouth. Suddenly, the woman rushed, trying to catch me off guard.

I lifted my fireplace poker like a baseball bat. The woman leapt toward me. I closed my eyes and swung as hard as I could. I felt the poker connect with a sickening thunk, the force of the blow throwing me off balance. I landed on my butt a few feet away. I opened my eyes, expecting the woman to be ready to pounce.

The woman had gone flying back from the impact as well. She lay on the floor, stunned. I was rather stunned myself. I was *so* not that strong. The solid iron poker was bent near the middle. I held it up in front of my face and stared at it, not entirely sure of what had just happened.

My opponent was down, at least for now, so I took the opportunity to rush to Jason's aid. I reached them in time to see Dan once again gain the upper hand in the fight. He pinned Jason much in the same manner as he had before. One of Dan's shoulders seemed to be dislocated, the hand of that arm had reverted back to human form and hung limp at Dan's side. Dan cocked back his good arm, that hand still in claw form. He poised it above Jason's throat. It all seemed to go in slow motion.

I hit Dan in the head with my crooked poker as hard as I could. He stumbled off Jason and skittered away from me. Jason looked up at me in shock. Join the club.

Dan stood and he did not look shocked. He looked very, very angry. He glared at me through hooded eyes, panting like a bull ready to charge. A trickle of blood dripped from his scalp and oozed down the side of his nose.

Jason struggled to his feet, his chest dripping a copious amount of blood. He stood by me, facing Dan, a united front. Dan looked across the room to his fallen companion. We had him outnumbered. He gave us a final look of pure hatred, then turned and ran out the front door, holding his limp arm against his side. What he wanted wasn't here anyhow.

Jason must have really been hurting, because he didn't go after him. I met Jason's eyes and began to take in the damage. His shirt was torn into bloody ribbons, completely baring his chest, where most of the damage was. Deep claw marks covered his chest and abdomen. White rib bones showed through some of the deeper scratches. I watched in stark amazement as the scratches began to heal themselves. It was like watching the scratches happen in reverse-motion, flowing together smoother than water.

Snapping back into action, I turned away from Jason and ran to Allison. I gently turned her onto her back and her eyes fluttered open. I let out a breath I hadn't known I'd been holding.

Jason came over and crouched beside us. He took one look at Allison's pale face, then turned to me with a meaningful stare. "She needs to go to the hospital."

"N-no," Allison mumbled. "I'm fine."

I met Jason's worried eyes, and couldn't help glancing down at his chest again. The scratches were nearly sealed, leaving behind bright pink welts that began to fade as well. "Go check on Lucy and Max," I told him, "I'll take care of Allison."

Jason's gaze crept over to the unconscious woman.

I'd forgotten about her. "It's fine," I told him. "Leave me your car keys and I'll get the cuffs we used on Lucy out of the trunk."

Jason nodded and pulled his keys out of his pocket, handing them to me, then in the blink of an eye, he was gone. I helped Allison to the couch then ran out to Jason's car to get the cuffs before our attacker woke up. I paused to look in the direction of Lucy's house, hoping to see, I don't know . . . something. She *had* to be okay.

I took a deep breath and turned my attention back to Jason's car. I examined the little electronic black square that dangled from the key chain and hit the button to pop the trunk. The cuffs were in plain sight, along with the chains we had used on Lucy. I noticed that the lanterns were gone and wondered if we had left them in the warehouse. I shook my head, trying to clear my thoughts. Maybe this was what it felt like to go into shock. I took another deep breath, then quickly grabbed the cuffs to rush back inside.

When I reached the living room the woman was still unconscious. I rolled her onto her stomach and cuffed her hands behind her back.

Allison was looking at me like she had never seen me before."Did you do that?" she asked. "Knock her out, I mean?"

"Yeah." I still felt numb, like I was watching everything from an outside perspective, not really involved in any of it. I noticed blood on the side of the woman's head. It had trickled to congeal in her long dark hair. I looked closer and realized that I had cracked her skull. I jerked my head away with a sharp intake of breath. I tentatively reached down to check her pulse, keeping my eyes off of her wound, but then jerked my hand back when I realized that I could see her breathing. I wasn't sure if that was a good thing.

Jason burst in through the front door, followed by Max. "Lucy's gone!"

17

"**W**hat do you mean she's gone! She can't be gone!" I practically screamed as I ran toward Max and Jason. I looked back and forth between the two of them, desperate for an explanation. She couldn't be gone. I finally focused on Jason as he began to speak.

"I found Max outside. He was unconscious. Wolf scent was everywhere, but it was not Dan's," Jason explained. "I went to Lucy's window. It was open and Lucy was gone."

"We were just a distraction," I said numbly, realizing that Dan had only attacked to keep us busy while Lucy was being stolen away. "H-how are we going to find her?" I asked, barely able to force the words out.

When Jason didn't answer me, I looked to Allison to see how she was taking the whole situation. She was sitting on the couch with her knees curled to her chest, not really looking at anything. Max went to sit down beside her.

Jason put his hand on my shoulder, turning my attention back to him. "We *will* find her," he said. "I promise."

"How can you promise!" I screeched without really meaning to. I went on a little more calmly, "You don't know that we'll find her. Dan has been one step ahead of us this entire time. We're playing his game and he has no rules."

"He's not going to kill her," Jason assured, "and I will not stop until we have her back." I didn't like how he said that Dan wouldn't *kill* her, rather than that he wouldn't hurt her. We couldn't stop him from hurting her. We needed to act. We couldn't waste any more time.

I stared at Jason and he answered my question without me having to ask it. "We at least have a place to start," he said calmly, and jerked his head toward the fallen woman, "if she'll talk."

I glanced at the woman, then back at Jason, meeting his blue eyes calmly, stare for stare. "She'll talk." I wasn't sure how I'd make her talk, but I was going to get Lucy back . . . one way or another. I shook my head at my thoughts. One day I was judging Jason for being a killer in his past, and now I was contemplating torture. Oh, how the mighty have fallen.

Jason was still watching me, waiting for me to explain my thoughts. I quickly looked away from his eyes and turned back toward Allison. "Allison?" I asked, not liking the fragile tone of my voice. She didn't answer. I walked to the couch and squatted in front of her. "Al? You in there?"

"She needs to go to the hospital," Jason repeated.

I looked back to find him kneeling by the unconscious woman.

"I-I just need a few minutes," Allison finally said, "then we'll go get Lucy back." I cupped my palms over Allison's hands warmly with an assurance I didn't exactly posses, then left her and went to kneel next to Jason.

"Why isn't she waking up?" I asked. What I thought was, *Please tell me I didn't kill her.*

Jason answered without looking at me, "She must be a newer wolf. She's healing the damage, but slowly."

Jason rose from the woman's side and came to face me. He put his hands on either side of my face. His wounds were gone, his bloody shirt and pants the only reminder that they had even been there. I stared at his chest, unable to get my thoughts straight. My world was still in a fog. I felt cold.

"Xoe," Jason said, turning my eyes up into his face. "I think you're going into shock."

I stared at his face, not comprehending his words. He pulled me against his chest and wrapped his arms around me. My entire body began to tremble violently. Jason lowered us down to the floor and lowered me into his lap. I breathed in the scent of vanilla and trees, cringing at the smell of blood that tainted it. My trembling began to subside as my body grew warmer. I felt safe. I knew it was an illusion, but it was one I was grateful for.

"She's coming to," I heard Max say.

Jason and I glanced at him in unison, then followed his eyes to the woman on my floor. She began to squirm around against her bonds.

Werewolves, even new ones, didn't seem to stay unconscious for very long. It was quite the time-saver. As the woman's senses returned, she started trying to scuttle away from us. I expected defiance, but instead she cowered, terrified.

"I-I'll talk," the woman stammered. "I can t-tell you where they are. D-don't hurt me."

Well that was easy.

Once the woman, Lela, got talking, it was hard to shut her up. Apparently Dan had been trying to gather pack members as he traveled. He'd go from town to town, looking for wolves that were like Max, rare cases that had survived without a pack. I guess they weren't as rare as we'd thought. He had only managed to acquire three pack members, including Lela. Lucy was Dan's first attempt at turning someone to be in his pack, to be his mate more specifically.

Whenever Dan would find a new wolf, he'd bring him or her into his "pack". Lela claimed that they didn't have much choice in the matter. It was hard for lesser wolves to resist an alpha, which Dan was. That was why most wolves went into packs willingly; their alphas would protect them from situations like this one. Dan had originally come to Shelby High to make Max join his pack, but he saw Lucy and things changed.

I looked down at Lela skeptically. "Why should we believe you?"

Her eyes widened even more, which a moment ago, hadn't even seemed possible. "I-I didn't want to join Dan. I had no choice, he would have killed me. He's like nothing I've ever seen, stronger and faster than he should be. I c-can tell you where he's hiding, where he'll take your friend."

I crouched down beside her. "Go on."

Lela told us that Dan was hiding at the old ranger station, roughly ten miles away from my house. It had been abandoned when the state built a new one a few miles east, about four years ago. So now we only had to go there, get past Dan and his other pack members, and get Lucy out. Ri-ight.

Jason, Allison, Max, and I got up to leave the room to discuss things away from Lela.

"Wait," Lela said, "there's something else."

We looked back at her expectantly.

"He wants Xoe."

What? "I thought I wasn't important, since I can't be turned," I said.

"He doesn't want to turn you, he wants to *use* you. He's obsessed with it. He thinks if he can find a way to control you, he can use you to solidify what he calls his *power base*. He's not exactly sane."

"Tell us something we don't know," I said, trying to act cool. On the inside I was shaking like a little girl.

We left Lela and went outside into the chilly night.

"Sooo what's the plan?" I asked Jason, as we all walked a little ways away from my house. We stood enveloped in soft moonlight that cast ominous shadows all around. I couldn't help trying to see through the shadows for any sign of eavesdropping werewolves.

"Can't we just call the cops?" Allison blurted before Jason could answer.

"And tell them what?" Jason replied. "That they need to go in armed with bazookas? Even if they did, their reflexes would not be quick enough. We would be sending them to die."

"Ok," I said, "there are three of them: Dan, and the other two pack members. Including Lucy, there are four of us."

"Five," Allison chimed in.

"Sorry Al, you don't really count."

She pouted, so I humored her. "There are *five* of us, including Lucy. So, we just need to reach Lucy, and we should have no problem getting back out, five against three."

"It's too dangerous," Jason countered. "I'll call Dan's old pack. For this, they will come. In the meantime I will try to stall Dan, and I will go alone,"

"Oh no," I replied. "You aren't pulling any of that gallant hero stuff with us. I, for one, refuse to be left out of the rescue."

"Me too," Allison chimed in.

"Me three," added Max.

"Then it's settled," I said, turning back to Jason. "We go in together."

Jason shook his head. "You could all be killed. He's not going to kill Lucy, but I don't think he will be as considerate with any of us. It's too risky."

"It's even *more* risky with just you going in," I replied. "At least with all of us we have some chance of success. How long will it take for Dan's old pack to get here?"

Jason met my eyes and tried to stare me down. I slowly crossed my arms and tilted my head to the side, staring back. Allison and Max came to stand on either side of me and mimicked my stance. Jason slowly nodded his assent, but he did *not* look happy about it. Too bad he didn't have a choice.

Jason sighed. "Okay, here's the plan . . . "

The plan was that we would take Lela, in cuffs, with the pretense of making a trade. We knew Dan would never go for a trade, but if we could distract him with conversation, maybe one of us could get near Lucy and free her from any restraints she might have. The idea was that no matter what happened, Lucy would have as much chance of escape as the rest of us.

I was trying really hard not to think about the

chance that we might not all escape. In the meantime, should we fail, we would hopefully have Dan's pack riding in to rescue all of us. They were based in Utah, so they would have to fly. If they were able to get an immediate flight out, we would still have two to three hours before they arrived.

We went back inside and Jason went into the kitchen to call the alpha of Dan's old pack. I listened to Jason's side of the conversation as he detailed all that had happened. After a few minutes more, I heard the phone click into the cradle.

Jason came back into the living room. "They're coming."

Max cleared his throat, turning everyone's eyes to him. "What about me and Lucy? Will they make us go with them?"

Jason didn't answer, instead he said, "You don't have to come with to the ranger's station, Max. You can just go home now."

Max crossed his arms at the wrists, then drew them to his sides, like an umpire calling someone out. "No way. I'm coming. We'll just have to worry about the pack when the time comes."

It was settled. We gathered Lela up and trooped out the front door, faces stern and somber: a vampire, a human, a teen wolf, another wolf who was terrified enough for the rest of us, and a half-demon without a clue. Bad guys beware.

18

There is a bumpy mountain road leading to the old ranger's station. We were all piled into Jason's car, bouncing as we crawled along. I was in the front passenger seat with my trusty fireplace poker across my lap. Lela was in the back, sandwiched between Max and Allison. Allison had traded in her not so effective pepper spray for a baseball bat we had found in my garage, though that probably wouldn't do her much good either.

I kept having to remind myself to breathe. My love for Lucy was all that kept courage running through my veins. The closer we came to our destination, the less confident I felt in our ability to pull off the rescue. Despite Jason's assurances, I wasn't convinced he could take Dan in a one-on-one fight.

Jason claimed that vampires were simply stronger than werewolves, though he did admit that Dan was stronger than any other werewolf he had ever met, confirming Lela's claims. It wasn't just Dan's fighting skills that made him dangerous. Dan had more physical strength and speed than he should have, than any werewolf should have.

As for Max, I was even more worried. The unknown, at least to us, pack member had bested him pretty easily outside of Lucy's house. Max claimed that his opponent got downwind and snuck up on him, but that fact alone made me think that Max wasn't a match for him.

I was the wild card in the situation. Including me, we were three against two, given that we couldn't trust Lela to join in the fight and Allison wouldn't be much help. I was stronger than I used to be, but I wasn't sure by how much. I didn't think that I could trust my newfound strength in the upcoming battle. I'd proven that I could deal a hit, but taking one, well . . . I was not looking forward to finding out how that would go.

"Please don't give me back," Lela urged, breaking the silence and my train of thought. "I can't go back to him."

"We're not going to *give* you back," I said. "You're just an excuse to get inside."

"But what if you lose? He'll take me back! I can't go back!"

I'd had enough. I took off my seatbelt and leaned into the backseat, getting in Lela's face. "You helped Dan attack us. As far as I'm concerned *you're* the reason he has Lucy. Now you're going to help us get her back, and just be happy that you're still alive."

Lela cowered and pressed herself back against her seat as much as possible, hiding behind her long, dark hair, trying in vain to distance herself from me.

"Calm down Xoe," Jason said in a voice that was meant to be soothing. He had replaced his ruined shirt with a dark green cotton t-shirt from his trunk. Max and Allison had frozen in place, each shoved as far away from me as possible.

I glared back at Jason, a snarl on my face.

He spoke slowly, "Remember what happened the last time you lost your temper?"

I couldn't think. All I felt was white-hot rage. It felt like burning embers were eating me up from the inside. This wasn't what usually happened to me when I got angry. This was something new.

"Remember what happened with Brian?" Jason urged just as calmly.

The memory of Brian's scared face came flooding back to me, sobering me and chasing away my anger, most of it anyhow. My temper had never been this bad, not even close. It was an all-too real reminder of my ... heritage. I sank back into my seat and crossed my arms, embarrassed by my outburst.

The bouncing of the car lessened as we began to slow. Jason pulled off to the side of the narrow road and stopped the car out of sight of the ranger's station. If a large enough truck came by, it wouldn't be able to fit past. Luckily, no one came up this way anymore.

Jason turned in his seat to look back at Allison. "You are going to wait in the car, in the driver's seat, in case we need to make a fast getaway."

"No way!" Allison argued. "You guys are *so* not going in there without me!"

"It makes sense Al," I said, trying to placate her, because I agreed with Jason, "you'll do us more good out here."

It was better for everyone if Allison stayed outside. She would be out of harm's way, at least farther out of it than the rest of us, and we wouldn't have to worry about protecting her while we were trying to protect ourselves. I was reminded that *I* was supposed to protect myself, and my heart sped a little.

Allison's face contorted into an angry pout. "Fine." She was *not* happy, but I'd rather have her mad at me than dead.

We emerged from the car, Max holding onto Lela by her cuffs and me gripping my fireplace poker. As we began walking toward the hideout, the unusually warm air gave my skin an electric tingle. My earlier bravado with Lela had worn off. I was all nerves now. I stopped walking. "Umm, remind me again what the plan is?"

Jason stopped beside me, laying his hand on my arm, "You don't have to go in Xoe. In fact," he gave me a small smile, "I would prefer it if you didn't go in."

I took a deep breath. "I'm fine. Let's go." I was *so* not fine. What was I thinking? I didn't know how to fight. Until tonight, I had never even been in a physical fight with a human, and now I was expected to fight were-wolves with a fireplace poker? I looked up at the sky, trying to keep myself out of full panic mode.

The moon stood out in the middle of the darkness, still mostly full. Tall pine trees cast ominous shadows across the dirt road leading to the abandoned ranger's station. Another warm breeze blew my hair back out of my face. Sweat beaded on my forehead.

Jason's tall, shadowy form led the way toward the abandoned building. I was next, with Max following a few feet behind us, dragging Lela along. I could hear Lela muttering, "No, no, no . . . " under her breath. I had to admit, I sympathized.

We approached the small, log cabin style building. It looked dark and empty. Had Lela led us astray? I looked back at Max. He nodded, confirming that Dan's scent was in the area. Jason motioned for us to stop.

Jason crept forward to the wooden door. He paused, as if sensing something, then suddenly rammed his shoulder against the door. It flew open inwards, slamming on the wall inside. All was quiet. Jason stepped into the dark interior of the building. From where I was standing, it looked empty. The hair stood up on the back of my neck. This felt like a trap.

Jason whipped back toward us. "Max!" he shouted.

I looked back toward Max and Lela just as a dark

figure barreled into Max. Max, Lela, and the attacker tumbled into the bushes at the edge of the road, out of sight down the four-foot drop. I started to rush to the area where they had disappeared into the foliage, then paused in mid-motion at the sound of male laughter.

I turned back toward the ranger's station as a short, stocky man came sauntering around the side of the building. His shadowed face revealed a full beard and completely bald head. Small, beady eyes were swallowed by his protruding brow, emphasized by his lack of hair.

"Wow, I wasn't expecting you guys to be *this* stupid," the man mocked arrogantly in a gruff, scratchy voice.

"Were you expecting to be outnumbered?" I asked with false bravado.

"By the two of you?" the man laughed, "Sorry, no competition." He started to walk forward. "You think you scare me?" He chuckled to himself.

Jason stepped into his path. Jason spoke to me in a dead-pan voice, "Find Lucy." His eyes never left his opponent. "Go!" he shouted, just as the man rushed him.

I went. I ran into the ranger's station and began searching frantically, holding my fireplace poker ready to swing. The mostly bare room was still. I saw some dark shapes in one corner and ran to the largest shape, thinking it was Lucy. My heart dropped as the shapes revealed themselves as some bunched up tarps and half-empty gas cans. I checked behind the counter and in the small bathroom. Empty.

I backed into the main room and examined the floor. The moonlight shining in from the large wood-framed windows helped me to make out several sets of dusty footprints. One set led to the back door. I stopped to listen. I could no longer hear the sounds of struggle outside. I started to run back to the front door, but forced myself to stick to the plan. Our attacker's purpose was likely to distract us while Dan escaped with Lucy. I couldn't take that chance. I turned and ran to the back instead.

I stumbled out the backdoor into the woods. "Lucy!" I shouted. I started running down the trail that led away from the ranger's station. I continued shouting for Lucy as I ran. Drawing attention to myself probably wasn't the best tactic, but I couldn't think of how else to locate her.

Tree shadows played tricks on me, making me see hidden attackers at every angle. What if Lela had lied? Who knew how many wolves Dan had actually gathered? Suddenly, I was on the ground. A thrill of pain shot from my arm through my body. I raised my unhurt arm in weak defense as I waited for my unseen attacker to deal their next blow, but the blow never came. I struggled to sit up, looking for what had taken me down. There was a gnarled tree root sticking up in the middle of the trail. We had bad guys aplenty, and I was taken down by a tree root. I was afraid to look at my arm. I had a feeling it was broken.

There was a sound from within the trees to my left. I stayed sitting in the dirt and tried to calm the noise of my ragged breathing. I peered into the shadows in the direction that the noise had come from. "Lucy?" I whispered hoarsely through gritted teeth.

I heard the sound again, it was a soft whimper. I folded my arm gingerly against my chest, clenching my teeth against the pain. I struggled to my feet and followed the sound of the whimper, abandoning my poker in the dirt where it had fallen. I looked down to find that the underbrush had been trampled on one side of the trail. I ventured farther away from the hiking trail, following the trampled path. I stumbled through the vegetation, wincing each time a hidden root or rock jarred my arm, until I noticed a dark figure huddled on the ground.

I clumsily ran to the figure, keeping my hurt arm pressed against my chest with my good arm. Lucy was tied and gagged. Her restraints were only rope, not silver chains. I knelt beside her and she started whimpering again, eyes shut tight. She was still in the jeans and tennis shoes that she had been wearing earlier that night. Smartly, she hadn't dressed for bed, else she'd be out here shoeless and in pajamas.

"Lucy, Lucy it's me," I whispered.

"Oe?" she asked through her cloth gag.

"It's okay Lucy, you're safe."

I crouched next to Lucy and used my knees to keep my hurt arm pinned across my chest so I could use my good arm to untie her hands. I struggled with the ropes for several minutes, but was finally able to free her arms. Lucy rolled into a sitting position, ripping off her gag. She started working on the rope around her ankles.

"Where is everybody? Where's Dan?" she whispered frantically. "We have to get out of here!"

"I know," I whispered back. "We need to be quiet, okay? Can you walk?"

"Yeah, I think so. I don't think I'm hurt." Lucy slowly rose to her feet. I carefully got up, bracing my bad arm against my stomach with my good arm again.

"What happened to your arm?" Lucy gasped.

"I fell. Can you help me tie it in place?" I glanced down at the rope that had bound Lucy.

She nodded, pulling off her hoodie. She picked up the rope and managed to *Macgyver* a makeshift sling for my arm. I closed my eyes and gritted my teeth together as she slipped the contraption around my shoulders. I had to squat down so she could reach behind my neck to gingerly tie the rope in place. As her wrists passed my face, I noticed raw rope burns around them. A pang of anger at Dan stabbed my stomach. I took a deep breath and managed to contain it, not wanting to lose my temper again.

"Is that okay?" Lucy asked, then before I could answer she added, "Where's Dan?"

I let all of the worry I was feeling fill my face. "I was hoping you could answer that. I thought he'd be with you."

Lucy shook her head. "The two guys that took me brought me straight here. I haven't even seen Dan."

I nodded. The two guys Lucy was referring to had to be the two that attacked us; the one that knocked down Max and Lela, and the bald man. That left Dan completely unaccounted for. "We have to go."

I crept back toward the ranger's station with Lucy following closely behind me. I tried to make as little noise as possible, but I felt dizzy and clumsy with pain. We stopped a short distance away from the dark building.

I turned to Lucy. "Allison is waiting down the road in Jason's car.Go wait with her."

"What are you going to do?"

"I have to find Max and Jason."

"I'm coming with you."

I gave her a worried look, but I knew the stubborn set to her jaw. It was a look that she, Allison, and I had in common, and Jason and Max for that matter. It was a wonder that our group functioned at all. Here's hoping we could all stay alive and continue to function.

Lucy was coming, and I had to admit I was glad for the company. We crept around the side of the station to the front door, where I had left Jason to face off with the bald man. The moon cast empty, still shadows all around. A chill crept up my spine. Something had gone terribly wrong. I should never have left them to fight alone. I crept to where Max had fallen into the bushes. Empty. That left the ranger's station.

I had a fleeting urge to run back to the car and Allison, drive away, and pretend like none of this had ever happened. But Jason and Max were here somewhere, hurt, or maybe worse. I tried to swallow the lump that had formed in my throat. Please don't let it be worse. They were here because of us. They came to save Lucy, to protect Allison and me. We couldn't leave them.

Taking a deep breath, I crept back toward Lucy and the ranger's station. Realizing my intent, she turned to walk into the building ahead of me. I saw movement on the other side of the door. "No!" I shouted, just as arms reached out and pulled Lucy inside. She let out a small scream that was cut off as soon as she disappeared into the darkness.

It was just like the stupid people that get killed in the horror movies. The whole time, you're shouting at the screen, telling them to run and call the cops. Whatever you do, you should never go back into the creepy dark building. Well, I was going in at full speed. I skidded into the building and came to a halt. I spun around just as the door slammed behind me. I was face-to-face with more features I didn't know. Dan's third pack member.

The man was tall and dark. He leered down at me with nearly black eyes, holding Lucy tightly against his chest with one hand clamped over her mouth. He didn't seem to notice her struggling and kicking against him. He smiled at me, revealing large, square teeth. Dan's voice behind me brought my attention back to the room.

Max was lying in the back left corner with the tarps and gas cans that I had mistaken for Lucy earlier.Lying *very* still. What I could see of Max's face was covered in purple and black bruises, his mouth swollen and bloody. Jason was in the opposite corner with his back to the room. What I assumed were Lela's cuffs were now around his wrists. I had no idea how they had unlocked them given we'd left the key at my house. Jason was just as still as Max. I looked around the room for Lela, and noticed a wolf peeking out from behind the counter. It had to be Lela. I *hoped* it was Lela, and not the bald man. Either way, we were missing one person. The wolf looked terrified, if a wolf could look terrified.

I turned to Dan, who was still dressed in his black outfit. "What do you want?"

"Well," he replied. "I originally wanted to just take Lucy and be on my merry way. I had no intention of hurting you or your company, but you left me little choice. Now, because of all of the trouble you and your little friends have caused me, I want more. Your vampire killed David, and you managed to turn one of my pack members against me. Lela shifted and fought against Brent when we attacked. She seemed to think that you and yours would save her. I had to show her how very wrong she was."

I guessed Brent was the man holding Lucy, and David had to have been the bald man. Dan started pacing with his arms clutched behind his back, chuckling to himself, like the mad scientist in a horror movie. He had totally lost it. He asked me, "Would you like to hear my new plan?"

I glared at him.

"I will no longer simply take my dear Lucy and leave the rest of you alone. I will still take her of course, but now I will take you as well. There's more to you than you've led us all to believe. I've come to my own conclusions on what that is, but we'll have plenty of time to prove my theories true or false once we get out of town. As for the rest of your party, they will all have to die. And little Lela? Do you wonder why she is still in wolf form? We'll have to dispose of the bodies somehow." Dan walked closer and got in my face. Sweat had beaded on his brow and began to drip down around his crazed features.

I turned my nose up and peered at him with prideful eyes.

"Ah," Dan said. "I see I've sparked your temper. Don't want to do that 'till I've got you on a leash. Are you surprised that I know? It really wasn't all that hard to figure out."

"I don't know what you're talking about," I said coldly.

"Tsk, tsk," Dan went on. "No more playing dumb, Xoe. I've figured it out, that elusive smell, you smell like *demon*."

"And how would you know?" I asked, fear leaking into my voice.

"Oh, I know all about demons, all about dealing with them too. Part of the draw of Shelby is its graveyard, perfect for calling on demons. You see, it's not only the size of a graveyard that makes it a proper catalyst for magic, but the age as well. Shelby's cemetery has both size and age, but that's a story for another time. We'll have plenty of time for that later. If you're a good girl, I'll give you any answers you might want."

I needed to keep him talking. I had to buy some time. Dan's pack *had* to be here soon. I asked conversationally, "But graveyards aren't evil are they? Why are they a good place to call demons?"

Dan smiled. "They're good for all sorts of stuff. Magic tends to collect in cemeteries. Raw power. I don't know the exact how and why, but the older and larger the cemetery, the more power that collects there." Dan began to pace with his arms clutched behind his back again. "The ritual needed to call a demon requires quite a bit of power, and with no magical talents of my own, I must rely on cemeteries."

I nodded. "But why would you want to call a demon?" I saw Max shift position slightly, gaining consciousness. I kept my eyes on Dan, urging him to continue.

Dan grinned like a teacher, proud that his pupil had asked a good question. "There is much to be gained in dealing with demons: strength, wealth, information, though there is much to lose as well. I've done pretty well so far. I may have even come across your father at some point. I'm guessing that he is your demon parent. Your mom doesn't have that particular smell. We'll eventually find out who he is. I can only imagine what he would trade for you."

I smiled bitterly. "He left when I was born. He obviously doesn't want me."

Dan chuckled again. "Well of course he didn't want you then, you were useless. But I imagine you have at least begun to come into your powers, after what you did to Lela. *That,* makes you far more appealing. He'll trade, and you will be reunited with dear old daddy."

Tempting as that offer was, I had no intention of meeting my dad. Dan's pacing had taken him closer to Max, leaving his back to me. I had to act, but what could I do? Suddenly, the door swung open and a loud crack resounded behind me. I spun around to face Lucy and the man called Brent. Brent had dropped Lucy to the ground, where she crouched, surprised. Allison was standing behind Brent's broad back, holding her baseball bat ready to swing again. Brent turned and grabbed for Allison, and Lucy jumped on his back. The three of them went tumbling out the door.

Arms grabbed me and threw me against the wall

again. A new shock of pain shot through my arm as I fell to the floor. Bright splotches blurred my vision as I tried to catch my breath. I opened my eyes to see Dan's red, hateful face inches from mine.

He spat his words into my face. "I'm going kill all of your little friends while you watch. Even my dear Lucy. I've grown tired of her antics. And your vampire? His death will be special. Nice and slow. I may even make you help with that one. I won't kill you though. I may even let you go. I'll let you live out your sorry little life with the memory of watching your friends die. I'll let you live with the knowledge that you did nothing to stop me. You are powerless. A worthless . . . little . . . nothing." His anger had flipped a switch in his mind. It was like he had two different personalities . . . as if the situation could get any worse.

Brent came limping back in holding Lucy in his arms. I didn't see Allison with them. I tried to struggle to a sitting position, but my body screamed with pain. My arm felt like it was made of fire. To look on the bright side, at least I hadn't been knocked unconscious from hitting the wall as hard as I did. Hoorah for superhuman strength.

Dan stalked to the other side of the room and grabbed Jason by his cuffs. He dragged Jason across the floor and threw him next to me. Jason had apparently come to.

He looked at me with defeated blue eyes. "I'm so sorry Xoe," he whispered.

"Shut up!" Dan shouted. He walked to Jason and kicked him in the stomach.

Jason didn't so much as grunt in response. He kept his eyes locked on mine.

Dan sneered and got back in my face. "How shall we kill him?" Dan stood back up and kicked Jason in the face. Fresh blood poured from Jason's nose to splatter on the floor.

My vision went red. I felt my blood boil. Hot rage washed through my veins, numbing my pain. I welcomed it with open arms. I wasn't afraid of my new temper anymore. Anything to wash away the image of Jason's bloody face.

I thought of Allison unconscious on my floor after Lela threw her. I thought of Lucy, screaming as her bones cracked and reformed her into a wolf. I thought of Max, his black and blue face against the floor. I thought of never seeing any of them again.

I let the rage wash over me. I reveled in it. Gathering my strength I lunged for Dan, not sure of my intention. My good hand had barely made contact with his chest when he erupted in blue-white flame. I threw myself backward and fell back against the wall. The fire crept up his shirt and began to turn to orange as the clothing burned. Dan dropped to the ground and started rolling, grunting in pain. The flames began to go out. I closed my eyes in defeat, waiting for the next blow.

I reopened my eyes to see a dark shape fly across

the room, spewing liquid. It landed on Dan. I smelled gas. Max had opened one of the gas cans and thrown it when he saw the flames. Within seconds, Dan was engulfed in fire. He started screaming. He continued rolling on the ground, a few feet away from me, but he couldn't put the flames out. The acrid smell of burning flesh began to fill the room. His screaming became something shrill, almost inhuman.

I looked to the front door. Lucy and Brent had disappeared. I couldn't make myself move to find them. A wolf's face appeared around the writhing, flaming mass that was Dan. Lela crept up and laid her large wolf head in my lap. Jason had struggled closer to lean against me in a half-sitting position, blood still dripping from his nose. The room began to fill up with putrid smoke. Movement at the door caught my eye. Lucy stood holding Allison up, silhouetted by the moonlight and blurred by smoke, with Allison's arm across her shoulders. I turned my attention back to the burning mass. Dan had stopped screaming. I should have been scared. I should have been horrified.

I numbly looked past the flames to the faces of my friends and stroked the fur of the wolf that sat calmly at my side. Lucy and Allison looked horrified. Jason carefully avoided my gaze. I realized that I was smiling. I had set a man on fire. I wasn't scared, I wasn't horrified. I was glad. He had hurt my friends. Burn baby, burn.

19

Max had disappeared. I looked away from the disbelieving faces of my friends toward the back door, wondering where he'd gone. He came limping out of the small bathroom, carrying a fire extinguisher I hadn't noticed earlier. He shuffled up to the burning mass formerly known as Dan. He sprayed *it* with the extinguisher, putting out the last of the flames.

Lucy and Allison stumbled past me, to stand behind where I was sitting. I followed their eyes to the front door of the ranger's station to see a tall, dark man framed by the light of the moon. For a moment I thought it was Brent, but then the man stepped forward, revealing strong Hispanic features framed by dark, straight hair reaching well past his shoulders. He had to be Dan's old alpha.

"Abel," Jason said in greeting.

The man, Abel, nodded his head in acknowledgment. His voice was a deep bass rumble. "I see that we were a bit late."

"You can say that again," I mumbled, thinking that he wouldn't hear me.

He whipped his head in my direction. "Excuse me?"

My eyes widened in surprise. Damn that supernatural hearing. It took me a moment to speak. "Nothing, um . . . sir."

He nodded and turned back to Jason. "I apologize for your troubles. You will be compensated fairly. As a favor, I will ignore the three living werewolves in this room that are not of a pack. But they should be warned, that three wolves constitute a pack on their own. If they are all to remain in Shelby, they must file the proper forms."

I raised my eyebrows. I had imagined the forming of a werewolf pack as something mystical with loads of ritual and traditions. Filing forms just seemed so . . . mundane.

Abel continued, "Now I suggest you all leave this place. We will dispose of the remains of the deceased."

"Thank you," Jason replied simply. His nose had stopped bleeding. He waited as Max approached with a set of handcuff keys. I didn't know where Dan had gotten them, but it sure was convenient. Max freed Jason's hands, then Jason got to his feet and slowly lifted me in his arms.

Lucy and Allison came to stand beside us. We made our slow progression outside, Max and Lucy trying very hard not to make any eye-contact with Abel. Lela followed at my heels, still in wolf form.

The cool night air was refreshing after being in the smoky interior of the ranger's station. "I can stand," I told Jason.

He slowly let me down from his arms, but kept a hold around my waist so I didn't fall. The woods to either side of us were alive with the movement of the other wolves from Dan's former pack. I glanced up at the moon as I shook bits of ash out of my hair, not allowing myself to consider where the ash had come from.

We limped and hobbled back down to the car where we took an assessment of our injuries. Miraculously, I seemed to be the only one with a broken bone, though everyone else had a lot more cuts and bruises than me. Jason, Max, and Lucy had already started to heal, though Lucy was healing at a slower rate. The bruises on Max and Jason's faces were already fading into a sickly brown edged by yellow. Allison was not so lucky. Her entire back was a swollen purple mess and she had several gashes on her arms. Apparently Brent had thrown her into some bushes and decided the fight was over.

Lela, still in wolf form, had walked down beside me until we reached the car, making sure I didn't fall. After we verified that we would all survive, I eased myself

into the front passenger seat, then turned to acknowledge her. She licked my hand, the one attached to my
unbroken arm. I gave her a pat on the head before she
turned and disappeared into the darkness of
the woods.

With everybody loaded into the car, it was time I
got to the hospital to have my arm examined. I was also
healing a lot more quickly than I should have been,
and Jason was worried that my broken bone would re-
knit itself before a doctor could set it. I was able to
convince Allison that she should get checked out as
well. She was, after all, only human.

We drove back down the mountain, reeking of
smoke. No one seemed to know what to say. What do
you say after a kidnapping, a supernatural battle, and a
murder or two?

"I smelled the gas, but how did you guys light Dan
on fire?" Allison asked.

No one was answering. I sighed. "It was me."

"You mean . . . "

"Yeah, my demon powers strike again," I said
bitterly.

"You weren't the one who killed him, Xoe," Max
interrupted.

"I set him on fire and he burned to death. Yeah, I'd
say I killed him."

"I got him with the gasoline," Max explained.
"Don't blame yourself."

I didn't answer. I appreciated Max's valiant gesture,

trying to take the blame, but I knew otherwise. It was my fire that had killed him, even if Max's gasoline had helped. I didn't really feel guilty. Dan totally had it coming. It was more the lack of guilt that was bugging me. I was already struggling with my loss of humanity in finding out about my heritage. Now I felt less human than ever.

We pulled into the hospital parking lot a little after 2:00 am. Our absolutely genius cover story was that Allison and I had fallen down the stairs in the house. Whatever . . . it would work. If anyone asked about our unpleasant odor, we'd play dumb. Allison and I got out of the car and headed into the hospital. Jason was going to get Lucy back home. If her kidnapping had woken her parents up, we would have a lot of explaining to do. We'd just have to hope for the best.

Allison and I got signed in at the front desk of the emergency waiting room. They insisted on calling our parents since we were both minors. Our moms were on their way, though it would take my mom several hours, seeing as she had to come from Washington. The doctor called me in first, deeming my injury the more serious one. My arm was in fact broken, my ulna to be more exact. The wonderful, wonderful doctor gave me pain medication and went about setting my arm and cleaning the various scrapes on my arms and back.

Eventually I went back into the waiting room, fresh plaster cast on my arm, to find Allison and her mom waiting. Her mom peered at me with her honey brown eyes disdainfully. My mom was still absent.

"What's your prognosis?" I asked Allison, trying to ignore the less than happy look her mom was directing at me.

"Some pretty major bruises, got a few stitches. Other than that, I got off pretty easy. The doctor gave me some pain meds." Allison was acting like nothing was wrong, but the way she avoided direct eye contact with me gave her away.

With that, Allison's mom stood and whipped her blonde hair in a perfect imitation of Allison, or maybe Allison's was an imitation of her mother, and they left me alone in the waiting room.

The hospital had decided that they weren't going to release me until my mom came to pick me up. Gre-at. I sat down in one of the uncomfortable plastic chairs and prepared to wait.

Several hours later, my mom gently woke me up. A word of advice, never sleep in plastic chairs. I hurt everywhere. Of course, that was probably mostly from the beating I had taken. She hustled me out to her car where I instantly fell back asleep. The next thing I knew I was in my bed. I didn't remember getting home. A dark form was seated in a chair next to me. Noticing that I was awake, the form stood to hover over me. Jason's face came into focus.

"Lucy?" I mumbled.

"We got her home safe. Her parents never even woke up. Apparently our luck held."

I tried to nod, but stopped because it hurt. "It's over?" I asked.

"Yeah," he said, sitting on the bed beside me. "I can leave town now, and let you get back to your life. Max will be here to help Lucy. But . . . if you want me to stay, I can, at least for the time being."

"Stay," I mumbled, before slipping back into darkness.

20

Sunlight streaming in through my window woke me. Jason was still sitting in his chair. I felt miraculously better. Maybe being a half-demon wouldn't be so bad. The extra healing power sure didn't suck.

"Morning," I said, turning my head toward Jason.

"Morning."

I looked at the dirt on my visible skin. I scrunched my nose. "I'm going to shower."

Jason smiled. "I was going to recommend that."

I gave Jason a dirty look, then went into the bathroom, shutting the door behind me. My mom had left a wad of plastic shopping bags and a roll of masking tape next to my sink for putting over my cast while I showered. I turned on the water to let it get hot while I bagged up my arm. When I was sealed up and ready to go, I slipped off last night's clothes and stepped under the stream of steamy water.

The water that sped toward the drain was tinted with dirt. Ick. I would need to wash my sheets today. I started to one-handedly lather shampoo in my hair and could no longer avoid my thoughts. Lucy was a werewolf. There was a vampire waiting in my bedroom. I was part demon. I had killed someone.

I let the water stream over my face to wash away my silent tears. I didn't know why I was crying. I felt numb. We were all safe now. We had all gotten out alive. That was what mattered. I clung to that thought in order to drown out everything else.

I finished cleaning all of the dirt off me, turned off the water, then wrapped my fluffy purple towel around me to step out of the shower. I approached my mirror and cleared a circle in the condensation. I expected to look pale and fragile, like I had many mornings recently. Though I did have some serious circles under my eyes, I didn't look fragile. I looked, and felt, strong. We had won.

As I finished my reverie in the mirror, I turned to survey the bathroom, realizing that I had forgotten to grab a change of clothes. I re-wrapped my towel tightly around me and opened the door to my bedroom. Jason very carefully avoided looking at me while I shuffled through my closet looking for something to wear. I didn't really care if he saw me in a towel, but I appreciated the sentiment nonetheless. I grabbed the deep red, long-sleeved shirt that Allison had picked out for me and one of the few pairs of non-holey jeans from my closet, went to my dresser to get underwear, then went back into my bathroom to change.

I had some difficulty pulling my casted arm through my shirtsleeve, but finally managed. I left the sleeve scrunched up to my elbow above the cast, then went back into my room. Jason was standing by the window, looking outside.

"I better go talk to my mom," I said.

"Do you want me to leave?" he asked, without taking his gaze from the window.

"No, I'll be back up in a sec." I left my room and gently shut the door, then trudged downstairs to face the music.

I expected my mom to be mad at having to cut her trip short to bail me out of the hospital, but she was all sympathy. She had actually baked blueberry muffins while waiting for me to wake up. She ran up and hugged me as soon as I came down the stairs, then hustled me to the table. There was already a coffee mug waiting for me as she went into the kitchen to grab the muffins and the coffee pot. She set the pot beside my cup and set a blue ceramic plate with three gargantuan muffins on it in front of me.

"Umm, am I expected to eat all of those?" I asked sarcastically while filling up my mug with coffee with my good hand.

Ignoring my question, my mom sat down across

from me. "So, I've been thinking, maybe I shouldn't go out of town so often anymore?"

"Why?" I asked, mouth full of muffin.

"You broke your arm and I wasn't here!" she shouted, then covered her mouth in surprise at her reaction.

"Wooaah," I said, waving my good arm in a calming gesture. "It's not that big a deal." I held up my casted arm. "It'll be good as new in no time."

"And how did it happen that Jason was around at two in the morning to take you and Allison to the hospital?"

"Um, we called him? Duh."

"Yeah, likely story," my mom said, smiling. "If boys are going to be hanging around, we need to lay down some rules."

I groaned at the mention of rules.

"First," she began, "I will be informed whenever you will be spending time outside of school with a boy. Second, when said boy is involved there will be a 9:00 curfew."

This elicited another groan from me.

"And finally," she went on, "know that you can always talk to me about anything pertaining to boys or otherwise. Now eat your muffins."

Unable to help my smile, I obliged and took another enormous bite. Mmm, muffins. Nice, normal, non-portentous muffins.

After breakfast, I went back up to my room to talk

to Jason. As I walked into my room I saw that he had returned to sitting in my desk chair. He looked up from my copy of *On the Road*, by Jack Kerouac. I walked over to my bed and plunked down. Jason looked at me expectantly.

"Sooo," I began, "we haven't heard anything from Lucy or Al since last night?"

"I haven't," he answered. "Perhaps you should try calling them?"

"No. I don't know, I guess I'm afraid they won't answer."

Jason's face scrunched up in confusion.

I elaborated, "Allison wouldn't meet my eyes the whole time we were at the hospital, and Lucy never even spoke to me after what happened with Dan. It felt like . . . like they were afraid of me." I could feel cursed tears welling up yet again. I kept my eyes very wide, trying to prevent them from falling. I didn't want to cry anymore. You would think I would have run out of tears by now.

Jason rose to sit on the bed and wrap his arms around me. My last thread of restraint dissolved and tears fell in hot streams down my face. Jason held me while I spilled what were hopefully the last of my tears for the situation. We ended up lying on my bed, dirty sheets and all, facing each other. Jason's greater height put his head a little above mine. My tears had finally run dry. He gently stroked my still-damp hair while I regained my composure. He smelled clean. He had showered at some point, but I wasn't sure when. I thought about all that Jason had done for my friends and me. He had risked his life for us. Somewhere along the road I had gotten over the fact that he was a vampire and had killed people in the past. After all, I was a killer now too.

So I decided vampire-schmampire. I looked into his dark blue eyes, leaned in, and kissed him for all I was worth. The kiss started out soft, he hesitated slightly. I wrapped the fingers of my good hand in his hair and pulled him closer, making him give in to the moment. He put his arms around my waist and pulled me against him and kissed me like he meant it. When he gently pulled away I was left flustered and without breath. He smiled a small smile and stroked the side of my face.

"You have visitors," he said. He gently kissed my forehead, and then, just like that, he was up and out the window. A heartbeat later there was a knock at my bedroom door.

"Come in," I called.

The door swung open and there stood Lucy and Allison.

Allison came hobbling into my room and gently climbed onto my bed beside me, obviously still in pain from last night. "Good morning sunshine," she said to me smiling. "Glad to see *you're* looking better. Non-human healing is *so* unfair."

Lucy walked over to my bed with lowered eyes, and

sat down beside me. When she finally met my gaze, there were tears in her almond eyes. I waited for her judgment, waited to be called a murderer, a monster.

"Thank you," She said.

I looked a question at her.

"You saved me Xoe, you all saved me, but you most of all. None of us would be here if it weren't for you."

I closed my gaping jaw and grabbed Lucy in a hug. I let her go reluctantly. Allison scooted closer to the wall and I scooted to the middle of the bed, giving Lucy room to lie on my other side. We all lay there looking at the ceiling.

"So," Allison began, "now that you're a full-fledged half-demon and all, are you finally going to get over your hang-up about Jason's past?"

I turned my nose up. "I don't know *what* you're talking about," I said with a haughty air. I knew I'd eventually have to tell them about Jason and me, but for now, I could do without them making girly noises and kissy-faces at the mention of his name.

"Oh come on Xoe, he is *so* in love with you."

"You know what Al?" I replied, ignoring her statement. "I think maybe *you're* the demon."

With that we all burst into laughter, and for just a moment were able to forget that our lives as we knew them had been turned completely upside-down.

21

Jason had to leave town for a few days to report back to Dan's pack and get whatever they were supposed to pay him, and to fill out some forms of all things. I didn't ask how much he was getting. However much they gave him, it wasn't enough. He has since returned to Shelby and he's staying, at least for now. He got himself a nifty apartment and everything. I'm pretty ecstatic about it, though I'll never admit it out loud. The whole dating thing is kind of new territory to me, but I seem to be doing okay. I finally had to tell Lucy and Allison. They would have found out eventually. The teasing has been ceaseless.

Brian's still not talking to me. I'm afraid that he never will. I can't really blame him for not wanting to get involved. I'm sad about Brian, but at least I still have Lucy and Al . . . and Jason. Max still hangs around. He follows Al around like a lost little puppy, no pun intended. She pretends not to notice.

I'm still learning to control my powers. I've accidentally lit a few things on fire, but luckily nothing living. Hopefully my luck continues, not just with my powers, but with everything else. Fingers crossed.

ABOUT THE AUTHOR

Please visit www.saracroethle.com for more information on this and other series by Sara C. Roethle!

SNEAK PEEK AT BOOK TWO!

I was sitting comfortably on the green love seat in my living room. Jason was beside me with his arm around my shoulders. I curled my legs up against his lap, content, then glanced over at the larger blue couch where Lucy, Allison, and Max sat.

In the few months since we'd met him, Max had managed to get us all addicted to watching soccer, which we were all doing now.

Suddenly, Max leapt out of his seat, spilling popcorn on the carpet. "Go! Go!" he shouted.

It was World Cup time, and the game was USA against Mexico. One of the USA players had the ball and was running ahead of all of the opposing team toward their goal. Now, I hadn't quite gotten a grasp on the rules yet, but I could tell this was a good thing. The rest of us jumped out of our seats and joined Max in cheering the player on. One of the Mexico Players was gaining on him.

"Ruuuun!" Max shouted while clamping his fingers onto his shaggy, sandy colored hair as if in pain. To say that Max was enthusiastic about soccer was an understatement. When you're around someone that devout, you can't help but get caught up in the excitement.

I watched the TV screen, unblinking as the Mexico player surpassed the USA player. Suddenly they collided and both went down. One of the refs came running up to the fallen players, blowing his whistle and yelling something at the USA player. The USA player got to his feet and started yelling back. Uh-oh. The ref whipped out a red card and threw the USA player off the field.

"What!" Max shouted, throwing his hands in the air. "That ref is delusional . . ." Max began a tirade, his pale green eyes squinted in anger.

I got caught up in the moment and started yelling at the TV along with Max, feeling a sudden surge of anger at what Max deemed an unfair call.

Then the TV exploded. Crap. Did I mention that I'm a half-demon?

The past few months had been eventful, to say the least. A stranger named Dan had come to town. He happened to be a werewolf. Because of him, my best friend Lucy is a werewolf now too. With the help of Max (also a werewolf), and Jason (vampire), we had managed to rid ourselves of Dan. I won't go into the grisly details on *how* we rid ourselves of him. Let's just say that the event made me question my moral fiber more than a little.

Amid all of this chaos, I found out that my dad, whom I've never met, is a demon, making me a half-demon. Demons aren't bad or anything. Well, not *all* demons are bad. At least, that's what Jason tells me. I have an inkling suspicion that he only says that to make me feel better. Yet, seeing as I'm the only demon I know, I'll just have to take his word for it.

At the explosion my friends all went completely silent, then turned in slow-motion to regard me as one. I looked back to the TV. The screen had completely shattered, and the frame was a charred mess. Heaps of black smoke poured out of its smoldering innards to fill my living room with an acrid stench.

I stood under the pressure of their gazes only long enough to turn on my heel and run across my living room. I went right out my front door, slamming it behind me. I heard the door open and shut again as I ran toward the tall pine trees that border my house. The scent of pine and crisp air hit me, instantly clearing my senses. I wasn't sure I wanted them cleared at the moment.

This had been happening to me a lot lately, the blowing up of random appliances thing. When my powers as a half-demon first manifested, I had burned my friend Brian just by touching him. Since then, I'd graduated to blowing things up or just lighting them on fire. My powers were related to my temper, and that temper was mighty hard to control these days. Even the most insignificant things could make me mad enough to do some real damage. I couldn't control it, and the threat of what could happen weighed on me constantly.

I stood trembling in the dark, silent trees, my arms wrapped tightly around me. I would not cry. I would not cry about the stupid TV. The moisture that I felt slipping down my face was simply a raindrop. Yeah, a raindrop, that's it. I heard footsteps behind me, then felt arms gently wrap around me from behind.

I leaned back against Jason's chest and tried to take comfort in his presence. I unclenched my arms and rubbed my hands across the blue flannel shirt that encased his arms. I felt a slight bit of tension leave my body, but not nearly enough.

"You don't need to be so upset about it," he murmured. "We all understand." Jason talks kind of funny, probably due to the fact that he was born in 1883. He had picked up on many of the nuances of modern speech, given the fact that he'd been around to see it evolve, but he'd spent most of his life as a vampire alone, so some words didn't sound quite right.

"I know you're all used to it by now," I said between sniffles. "I just hate not being able to control it. What if it's one of you next time?"

Jason squeezed me a little tighter, keeping me warm despite the fact that I was only wearing a gray cotton t-shirt and jeans in Oregon, in December. He brushed his lips against my cheek. "We must simply be sure that we don't make you mad," he said, trying to lighten the mood, "though it is a somewhat difficult task these days."

I struggled out of his arms and turned to point a finger in his smiling face. "This is no time to crack jokes."

He put his arms up in mock surrender. "Oh no! Don't burn me!"

I pouted as I returned my hand to my side. "I could, you know. I could hurt you, or Lucy, or Al, or Max."

Jason lowered his hands and took on a more serious tone. "You will not harm us. You have more control than you think. Otherwise, you would have blown me up a thousand times over."

I crossed my arms and pretended to consider what he'd said. I nodded. "True, very true."

Jason smiled. "Come now my little demon, back inside."

I stomped my sneaker-clad foot on the hard, damp soil. "Half-demon," I corrected sharply.

"Of course," he conceded. Before I could react, he picked me up and threw me across his shoulder to carry me back inside.

I fake struggled, shouting, "I'll burn you! Don't tempt me!"

Jason paused and hoisted me up, getting a more secure hold on me. "I am well and truly terrified." He easily held onto me with one hand while he opened the front door and walked us inside.

By the time Jason managed to plop me back down on the couch, Lucy had swept up all of the TV bits and was emptying the dustpan in the kitchen. Jason left me to help Max lift what remained of the TV frame to take it outside, where it would await a ride to the dump. Poor TV. I didn't know how I was going to explain this one to my mom. I mean, appliances only catch fire so often. The toaster and the washing machine had each already met their untimely demise.

Jason returned to sit beside me on the couch, wrapping his arm around my shoulders again. Allison came to stand in front of me while shrugging on her fake-fur lined coat. She pushed her long, honey blonde hair behind her ears, then leaned down and kissed me on the cheek. "We're taking off Xoe. Call me tomorrow."

I gave her a feeble wave goodbye. Lucy leaned over the back of the couch to give me a hug, enfolding me in her petite arms and long, pin-straight black hair. As soon as Lucy backed away, Max gave my shoulder a comforting squeeze, and soon I was alone with Jason. For a little while anyway. My mom would be home from doing her Christmas shopping soon.

I snuggled up against Jason's broad, muscled chest (not over-muscled mind you. I like my men lean). His hand lifted to stroke my pale blonde hair. It had grown long enough to brush past my shoulders. I was overdue for a cut.

I turned my head so I could look into Jason's deep blue eyes, and I do mean deep blue, like the color of the sky just before it turns to black. I'd never seen eyes that could be that dark and still manage to look blue until I met him. "Sorry I'm so messed up right now," I said quietly. "I just can't seem to get used to all of this demon stuff."

Jason smiled down at me warmly. "It's a lot to take in. You are doing well, given the circumstances."

I looked back down at my lap, feeling like a failure despite his encouragement.

Jason continued to watch me, being far too observant for his own good. "What's wrong Xoe? I can tell you have something to say."

I debated for a few seconds on whether or not I wanted to tell him. I sighed. Here went nothing. "The dreams started again."

Several months ago, before my life went to hell-in-a-hand-basket, I had started having these dreams, and I always awoke with a fever. I dreamed of fire, then I found out that I was part demon. A wolf was in one of my dreams, and my best friend got turned into a werewolf.

Once things had calmed down, I'd finally confided in Jason about the dreams. The only other people who had known were my mom and Lucy. Jason had instantly come to the conclusion that I had a minor gift at premonition, and it had come out in my dreams.

Jason's arms tightened around me slightly. "Tell me."

"Well," I began, "the fire's back, for starters, but this time none of my friends or family are there." I had seen my mom and my friends consumed by the flames in my previous dreams. "At first, I think that I'm alone, then I feel a presence at my side. I blink, and when I open my eyes, there is a man silhouetted against the flames. I can't see him, but I somehow know him. Then, he turns away from me and jumps into the fire."

Jason was silent for a moment. He snuggled a little closer to me, if that was even possible. "Do you have any idea what it means?" he asked finally.

I shook my head morosely. "Not a clue, but I don't like it."

"Nor do I," he replied quietly. "Have you told anyone else?"

I shook my head. "Nope. There's no sense in worrying the others. It could be nothing."

He gave me a very knowing smile. "Or it could very well be something. It can't hurt to have everyone on their guard."

"But on guard for what? We don't even know who the man in the dream is."

"All the more reason to be prepared for anything," he countered.

I pursed my lips into a pout. "So, in other words, you're not just going to let me ignore it in the hopes that it goes away?"

He grinned down at me. "Like you did with me?"

I shoved away from him playfully. "I did *not*."

"Yes, uh-huh," he replied. "You utterly refused to admit your feelings for me until after we almost died."

I raised my eyebrows coyly. "Who says I have feelings for you?"

He grabbed me and pulled me close again. "I'm a vampire," he answered dramatically. "We can sense these things."

Our banter was interrupted by the sound of a key in the door. A few seconds later, my mom walked in, hands full of shopping bags. She threw her bags on the floor and stripped off her khaki, knee-length trench-coat to reveal dark-wash jeans and a dark brown, cable-knit sweater. Her newly shoulder length, dark brown wavy hair blended into the sweater so that you couldn't tell where one stopped and the other began. She walked toward us and threw her coat across the back of the love seat. "Hey you two, what are you . . . where's the TV?"

I smiled nervously.

"Not again?" my mom sighed loudly in her rich, throaty voice. I like to lie to myself and pretend that my voice sounds like hers, but in reality mine's an octave or so higher. Though our voices are the least of our differences. My pale skinned, green eyed genetics were obviously not passed on from my mom's side. Our looks are on opposite sides of the color spectrum.

I nodded, while attempting to hold my nervous

smile in place. "I think, maybe, we have like, an electrical problem or something?"

My mom put her hands on her hips. "An electrical problem that causes household appliances to spontaneously combust?"

Jason and I both shrugged.

My mom stared at us skeptically, then turned to regather her shopping bags. I couldn't imagine what she actually thought about the exploding appliances. She had played it pretty cool so far, but her observant patience could only last so long.

My mom stopped to regard us again before she went up the stairs to her bedroom. "I'll call the electrician tomorrow." Then, when she reached the top she shouted. "And it's 9:00!"

9:00 was my *boy curfew*, 11:00 on weekends. After that, Jason either had to go home, or if we were out, I had to come home. Jason reached up and touched my face, gently guiding me toward him. He leaned forward and met my lips for a chaste kiss. His lips were warm and soft against mine. I lifted my arms to wrap behind his neck, twining my fingers in his tousled dark brown hair. The kiss turned a little less chaste. Before I knew it, I had scooted onto Jason's lap. His arms circled my waist and pulled me against him. I sank into his warmth, feeling my troubles melt away.

This was a relatively new feeling for me, feeling absolutely safe in someone's arms. My dad had never been around, and as hard as my mom tried, she just didn't really fit into the big, strong protector role. Up until now, I'd always felt that I simply had to protect myself. It wasn't a bad feeling, but it could be lonely. In other words, it wasn't about needing to be protected, I just enjoyed finally having the option. Our little session went on for a while longer, until I reluctantly pulled back.

I met his dark blue eyes again and almost dove back in for more. Sadly, I managed to restrain myself. "See you tomorrow?"

He gave me one more gentle kiss. "You could not keep me away."

He was up and out the door in 5 seconds flat. It still unnerved me how quickly he moved. It was even more unnerving when Lucy did it, though she wasn't as fast as Jason. I wasn't very fast at all, and not for lack of trying. Hanging out with werewolves and a vampire all of the time had brought me to the conclusion that I was the worst half-demon ever. I just couldn't compete.

During my reverie I checked to make sure that Jason had locked the front door behind him, which he had, as always, then I journeyed upstairs to my bedroom. I readied myself for bed in the adjoining purple themed bathroom, then changed into green flannel pj pants and an oversized David Bowie t-shirt. I sat down on my dark green comforter and hugged a yellow cased pillow to my chest. I was *so* not ready for bed.

I looked over at my computer desk with its backdrop of old-school horror movie posters, and contemplated surfing the web for a while. Finally, I settled on snuggling up in bed and reading my copy of Stephen King's *Desperation* that Jason had recently purchased for me. There was nothing in that book that would be more frightening to me than my dreams.

When I finally shut off the lights, I gave a weak prayer that I wouldn't visit any dark places filled with fire. Fat chance.

Printed in Great Britain
by Amazon

36746392R00138